A COVENANT OF SALT

MARTINE DESJARDINS

A COVENANT OF SALT

A novel

Translated by
Fred A. Reed and David Homel

Talonbooks
Vancouver

Talonbooks
P.O. Box 2076, Vancouver, British Columbia, Canada V6B 3S3
www.talonbooks.com

Typeset in New Baskerville and printed and bound in Canada.
Printed on 100% post-consumer recycled paper.

First Printing: 2007

The publisher gratefully acknowledges the financial support of the Canada
Council for the Arts; the Government of Canada through the Book Publishing
Industry Development Program; and the Province of British Columbia
through the British Columbia Arts Council and the Book Publishing Tax Credit
for our publishing activities.

L'évocation by Martine Desjardins was first published in French by Leméac Éditeur
Inc., Montreal, in 2005. Financial support for this translation provided by the
Canada Council for the Arts and the Department of Canadian Heritage through
the Book Publishing Industry Development Program.

Library and Archives Canada Cataloguing in Publication

Desjardins, Martine, 1957-
    [Évocation. English]
    A covenant of salt / Martine Desjardins ; translated by Fred A. Reed and
    David Homel.

    Translation of: L'évocation.
    ISBN 978-0-88922-566-4

    I. Reed, Fred A., 1939- II. Homel, David   III. Title. IV. Title: Évocation.
    English.
PS8557.E78284E9613 2007   C843'.54   C2007-901063-6

For Gabrielle
and in memory of Mary Evoy

I

MAGNUS McEVOY

The curtains were drawn in the manor house parlor, but the sun shone unhindered through their threadbare velvet. Judging by the dancing of the dust motes in the fetid air, it would have been the noon hour, though the small pendulum clock atop the writing desk, which had stopped around the time the ink had dried at the bottom of the inkwell, could not have testified to that. Standing silently at the threshold, holding between his flattened fingers the brim of a hat to which clung wisps of damp straw, Titus awaited the orders of Her Excellency, the heiress of the Armagh estate.

There had been a time when the parlor was draped in moiré, the same citron yellow as the sash with which Rear-Admiral Magnus McEvoy had been decorated in honor of the victory on the Plains of Abraham. The fabric lent a gay touch to the room, with the Waterford crystal candelabra and the watercolors of Irish landscapes. However, upon the death of her father, on May 20, 1791, Lily McEvoy (who had assumed his title of Excellency) ordered all these ornaments removed to the attic, at the same time as she relegated to disuse the dining room and the Rear-Admiral's former bedroom. She kept only a Celtic harp, a writing desk upon which a place would be set for her at mealtimes, and an armchair in whose cushioned depths she would pass entire evenings lost in somber thought.

"Do you know Master Anselm?" she asked Titus abruptly.

Her voice was piercing, raspy, the sign of impulsive temperament. It sent a shiver through the farmhand, who nonetheless held his peace. He seemed to balk at the question, perhaps because his clenched jaw gave him the restive look of the cattle among which he had been raised and which had long been his only company.

Lily McEvoy's hand had been hovering impatiently above the faded blotter; now it picked up one of the inkpots as if it were a stone she meant to hurl.

"Well?" said the heiress. "Answer the question!"

With great effort, Titus spoke.

"He is a stone carver. I met him once ..." Then he added, between clenched teeth, "When Your Excellency sent me to seek him out in the village of Beaumont, many years ago."

On that day, Titus had been summoned in all haste to the manor house. Intimidated at being admitted for the first time into the very precincts he had often spied upon from behind the bushes, through the lighted windowpanes, he had, as he entered into the parlor freshly hung in mourning, wiped his manure-clogged boots upon the edge of the carpet. With a sting of shame he still remembered the mocking smile, bordering on cruelty, on Lily's face as she handed him a letter. It bore the name of Master Anselm, and her only instructions to Titus, who had never learned to sign his name, were to deliver it to Beaumont.

"That was ten years back," added Lily. "Will you be able to find him?"

"If I recall properly, Your Excellency had given him permission to take up quarters in the hut, near the old salt mine."

"He is there still. I would like you to go there this very afternoon, and bring him here. You are to tell him that he is invited for supper. Repeat it; let us see if you have understood exactly what you are to say."

Titus had uttered not more than three words when Lily McEvoy dismissed him from her sight, ordering him with a shout to close the door behind him.

Once she was alone, she stepped over to the window and, with trembling hand, parted the drapes. Titus was making his way down the main walkway. She watched him as he went, not taking her eyes off him, and she did not move until long after he had disappeared into the copse.

"If only," she finally sighed, "I have not forgotten anything."

In preparation for Master Anselm's arrival, Lily had gotten up with the chickens. Her jaws which, in her sleep, she had clenched like an oracle grinding laurel leaves with a prophetic gnash, were tense and painful. She bathed them, dipping her handkerchief into the pitcher of salt water, then hastened to dress.

Clad in a simple black gown with a tulle modesty, she made her way stealthily down the staircase and towards the kitchen, as was her custom, hugging the walls of the long corridors, pressing her ear to the closed doors in hopes of overhearing a conversation or, at the very least, surprising the domestics. There were only two at the manor house: Perpetuity, who looked after the household chores, and Ursula, who was in charge of the ovens. Both were sturdier than oak trunks, and about as appealing to the eye. The Rear-Admiral, who had engaged them upon their discharge from the Quebec City foundling home, had demanded, in return for his hospitality, their loyalty and dedication—of which he would apprise himself by eavesdropping on them through tiny hatches pierced at strategic locations in the ceiling. Should they evince laziness or rebellion, he would not hesitate to threaten them with his trusty cat-o'-nine-tails, whose pitiless thongs had maintained discipline aboard his frigate, then in the salt mine at Armagh. The two maidservants were already in their forties when Lily inherited them. She substantially tempered the paternal methods, though by inherited predisposition she wielded a heavy hand, and dreaded mutiny above all else.

This time, her precautions were not in vain. When she burst into the kitchen, Ursula and Perpetuity were about to break maple sugar over their morning porridge. Lily forbid herself sweets in all forms, and believed that the rest of the household could do without them as well. She would authorize the purchase of molasses only for the preparation of cured meats, in the fall—causing no end of annoyance to the maidservants who had a weakness not only for sugar pie and maple-sugar taffy, but for jams and jellies, and griddle cakes with syrup. Once the maple sap began to run, with the melting of the snow, they would take to the deepest part of the woods and make sugar surreptitiously, in an abandoned hunter's shelter.

Caught in the act, Ursula and Perpetuity hastily stuffed the golden morsels into the pockets of their aprons and, in a single movement, snapped to attention in front of the fireplace, bonnets askew and features all but crystallized. To their good fortune, the copper pots had been scoured with coarse salt and vinegar the previous night, and they sparkled on their hooks. The massive cupboards, as well as the wood floors, smelled of fresh beeswax. The two had no cause for alarm. Her Excellency, who paused to scrutinize their bowls of sugared porridge with a squint of displeasure, had neither the intention to reprimand them, nor the time to carry out a general inspection. She had come to inform them that she would be expecting company that evening for supper.

News that the Rear-Admiral had risen from the dead would not have been greeted with greater incredulity. Ursula, her eyebrows raised halfway up her forehead, forgot her rapidly cooling breakfast. To the best of her knowledge—and, as chief cook, she was in a position to know—Her Excellency had not shared her table with anyone since taking possession of the Armagh estate. The closest neighbors, who had once been welcome, were shown the door in quick succession. The ties of friendship maintained by the Rear-Admiral and his wife were definitively broken off. As for the handful of visitors who would inadvertently come knocking on the doors of the estate—travelers who had lost their way, zealous road inspectors—they were never so much as allowed to cross the threshold. Father Compain would call on them once a year, generally at the end of the harvest to collect the tithe. He was an exception to the rule, though even he would only be served refreshments on the veranda—coltsfoot wine for the most part, accompanied by two or three oatmeal cakes. Who could have blamed him for staying only as long as was necessary to recall, with a lick of his thin churchman's lips, the delicacies that had once graced Her Excellency's mother's table? It had been an honor to share her braised goose with turnip fricassee, not to mention the syllabub that was "so light that it almost ate itself."

Whenever he spoke of the late and much lamented Laurence McEvoy, Father Compain would call her "our Distinguished Benefactress," for it had been she who prevailed upon the Rear-Admiral to donate the wood needed for the construction of a chapel on the edge of the Armagh township. Nor would he ever forgo an opportunity to associate her name with the prayers of the faithful as he intoned the invocation for the deceased. His intercession was all the more necessary, for the poor dear departed had not been laid to rest in consecrated ground, as was prescribed, but in an altogether profane corner of the estate. How often had Father Compain enjoined Lily to transport Madam McEvoy's remains to the church at Beaumont, where he had reserved for her a choice location under the center of the nave, to the right of the altar! It was all for naught. Despite his remonstrance, the young lady remained unmoved. If the Church would not allow her parents to be buried together, their bodies would remain at Armagh. Such was her decision. The discussion was closed, the audience had come to an end, and Titus was ordered to bring up the vicar's carriage. In the ensuing silence, he sipped the last drops from his glass with the resignation of an animal licking its wounds, raised himself painfully from his armchair, then made his way down the veranda steps, gripping the banister. As he was about to whip his horse, his arm fell to his side and he turned to Lily with a despairing look:

"Reassure me at least that our Distinguished Benefactress has not been laid to rest in the mine, as people around the county are saying."

Lily blinked not an eye, and without an answer, waved her hand in the vicar's direction. Then she vanished into the depths of the manor house, whose door slammed violently as though of its own will, with the full weight of its heavy panels, its bolts and hinges.

What didn't the people of the county whisper about the lady they called Black Lily? Some claimed she crept into houses in the wee hours to steal infants from their cradles, that she would slice them into small pieces and, like the innkeeper in the legend of Saint Nicholas, would layer them in her salting tub. Others related that her red hair had burst into flame as she was being baptized, just as Father Compain was sprinkling her with holy water. Ursula herself swore she had seen her with her own eyes, dancing with ghosts by moonlight. God forefend, those impious creatures might well appear at this supper. Perhaps they would be the only guests.

"The dining room has not been used for some time," observed Perpetuity.

"Ten years exactly," Lily replied. The room, naturally, would have to be opened and aired out without delay. There were carpets to be brushed with salt water to bring out the colors, mirrors to be dusted, furniture to be polished (not forgetting the knife case!), slip covers to be removed from chairs, the Irish linen tablecloth and the embroidered serviettes to be ironed, porcelain to be washed and silver to be shined, candles to be placed in the candelabrum. Don't forget to light a peat fire in the fireplace, for the nights were still brisk …

Perpetuity raised her hand to interrupt her:

"How many guests is Your Excellency expecting?"

She was unable to contain her enthusiasm. More naive than Ursula, she had quickly invested the dinner with hopes that the manor would, at long last, awaken from the torpor into which mourning had plunged it for all these years. Were Her Excellency prepared to throw open the doors of the dining room once more, the hunting parties and grand soirées could not be far behind. Visitors would once again parade through the parlor, laughter would once more set the crystal goblets tinkling, and the floorboards would echo to the sound of jigging feet. Eventually a suitor would come calling. For, when the Lord had said, "It is not good for the man to be alone," He had surely meant woman as well. True, Her Excellency was already twenty-seven years old, but it was not too late for her to bring an heir into the world.

Perpetuity had no sooner made her wish than the answer to her question brought her illusions to an abrupt end.

"You will set two places, at either end of the table," said Lily. "One for me, the other for Master Anselm."

At mention of his name, Ursula and Perpetuity exchanged knowing glances. They knew Master Anselm only by sight, but they knew where he lived, and the reprehensible penchant that led Her Excellency to his door every Friday, when she was supposed to be praying to the Blessed Sacrament ...

A few months after the death of the Rear-Admiral and the closing of the mine, while harvesting apples in the orchard, the two maidservants had, from their vantage point in a tree, looked on as the young woman set out for the chapel. Great was their surprise as they watched her turn onto the road to the mine, and vanish into the copse. Their curiosity aroused, they let the apples in their aprons tumble to the ground and, taking care not to rustle the dead leaves on the path, they followed Her Excellency to a clearing where the October sun cast its faint rays. Carrying a bundle under her arm, she was making straight for a tumble-down, whitewashed outbuilding covered with Virginia creeper. Pounding on the door, she called out the name of Master Anselm. A man soon appeared and relieved her of her bundle. From it he drew a loaf of bread, a bunch of carrots and a partridge. "So that," muttered Ursula, "is where the contents of our pantry have been disappearing."

The man was no longer in the prime of youth, and was slightly stooped. But he was so powerfully built, with his sturdy frame, his muscled neck, his broad shoulders and his outsized hands, that he still possessed all of youth's haughty vigor. His beard and close-cropped hair were dull black, like flint, while his eyes gleamed like the depths of a well. Taken aback, Perpetuity could not contain a stifled gasp. Leaning toward her ear, Ursula whispered that this man was the Devil incarnate.

Holding at arm's length a heavy pine-resin torch, he led Her Excellency a short distance up the Loutre River, to the foot of a clay mount. It was then that the two domestics caught sight, through the trees stripped bare of their leaves by the wind, of the yawning maw of the salt mine to which the Rear-Admiral had so often threatened to banish them. Terror overcame them. They turned back, but not before seeing Master Anselm take a liberty that was to be imprinted upon their memory with the same indelibility as the initials of the Armagh estate tattooed upon their forearms. At the very moment that Her Excellency entered into the cavernous orifice of the mine, the man reached out to steady her and grasped her by the waist, so that his heavy hand left its dusty imprint upon the cascade of black taffeta—a white, dimly scintillating signature. When Her Excellency returned to the manor house that evening, as dusk had all but fallen, that same dust covered her from head to toe. Perpetuity, who had the duty of cleaning her gown the following day, as well as after each of her mistress's escapades, had merely to touch the taffeta with the tip of her tongue to confirm what she already suspected: the cloth was permeated with salt. As to how such a thing had happened, she had long since formed her own idea. The rock-hard floor of the mine and Master Anselm's outsized hands played so overwhelming a role that she preferred not to think about it. And now, imagine! It was for this devil of a man that they must take the trouble of opening the dining room ...

The furtive glances of the two maidservants did not escape Lily, though she gave no indication of having noticed them. Instead, she turned abruptly to Ursula, and began to plan the evening meal.

"I could always slaughter a nice, fat capon," the cook suggested.

Her Excellency had nothing of the kind in mind. She had resolved to be patient on this day, but now she could not conceal her nerves.

"That will not be necessary. The provisions we have on hand in the salt room will suffice. Show me what is left."

With a frown, Ursula opened an iron door that creaked on its hinges. The salt room, just off the kitchen, was a kind of underground store whose walls were lined with blocks of salt to absorb the ambient moisture. Nearly depleted after the long winter, it held no more than a bear's ham hung from the ceiling, small chunks of pork belly, strips of deer meat and smoked partridge breast. The previous fall, Lily herself had prepared the mixture of salt, saltpeter and molasses to preserve the meats. Pushing aside a tub in which cabbage was fermenting in brine, Ursula came across several herrings, anchovies and a jar of pickled saltwort. For all the poverty of the victuals, Lily nodded in satisfaction.

"A bit of this and a bit of that will fill the bill," she decided.

As she closed the salt room door herself, she was overcome by a sudden dizzy spell, and had to seek out a chair. Ursula stepped forward to pour her a glass of water, but she waved the kitchen maid away. At her side, Perpetuity watched her closely out of the corner of her eye. She pondered her mistress's chapped lips, her split fingertips, her broken nails. Once so lustrous, her auburn hair was like straw. Suddenly a thought came to her with the full force of revelation.

"She is drying out from the inside. Like a bone gnawed to the marrow, like green birch consumed in fire. She doesn't drink enough and she salts everything, as Ursula herself says. The salt she's eaten is withering her skin. Already it has shriveled her heart. Her bust is hollow, she has never grown to maturity. Her pelvis is arid, her loins sterile. How long have I been doing her laundry, and never found a trace of blood?"

Yet the blood was flowing back to Lily's cheeks. She got to her feet, circled the kitchen twice, her hands clasped, then turned to Perpetuity.

"You will also clean my white gown," she instructed her. "Now, I must go up to the attic. Neither of you is to disturb me."

The maidservant seemed to detect, in her mistress's voice, a note of embarrassment. She watched as she left the kitchen, and with a sigh bit into a lump of sugar.

There was no ladder leading to the attic; rungs of thick rope had been rigged between five shrouds in the nautical manner so dear to the Rear-Admiral. Though she still felt a bit faint, Lily scaled them with the agility of a deckhand, clutching the hem of her dress between her teeth. No sooner had she raised the trapdoor than a whiff of stale, rank air assaulted her. Her breath came in shallow gasps.

"The embalmed whispers of the past," she thought as she pulled herself up through the opening by the strength of her arms.

Hidden from the prying eyes of indiscretion, the attic was built like the inverted hull of a three-master. Daylight, dilute and pallid, filtered through two scuttle-shaped windows at the far extremities, only to die out in a welter of sea chests, furniture and old tools. Not even a mother cat could have found her kittens there. Lily tiptoed down a passageway littered with dead flies, the fringes of her gown sweeping away their friable carcasses as she went, until she had completed her tour of the attic. Stopping in front of each object, she caressed it for a moment, then reluctantly laid it aside and moved on. It was as if she were trying to reacquaint herself with her own memories.

Lily had always taken pride, perhaps to excess, in her exceptional memory. It was true, nothing she had learned by heart was beyond her recall. She could recite the names of the seas, the straits and gulfs of the world, and those of the islands in order of size. She could declaim the answers to the four hundred and fifty-four questions of the catechism. She could retell the legends of Cuchulainn, Queen Deirdre and the Knights of the Red Branch. She could list the innumerable patronymics of her family tree, reel off the birth dates of all the saints of Ireland and the years of rule of the two hundred and fifty-three popes. She mastered the nomenclature of a ship's masts, yards, sails and stays, not to mention the date of Brian Boru's victory at Clontarf and of the defeat at the Boyne ... Unfortunately, this admirable faculty for storing knowledge whose interest was equaled only by its superfluity made Lily susceptible to the slightest diversion, perhaps because her storehouse was so selective. Her attention span was extremely brief. She would abandon books under the trees, leave her slippers beneath the table, misplace her combs behind cushions, discard her shawls pell-mell throughout the house, unable to remember where she had left them. Rifle through the closets, empty the commodes, reverse the mirrors though she may, she could never lay hands on the objects that, by purest malice, constantly eluded her. Had Perpetuity not been picking up behind her, she would have lost everything.

The attic, though, was her private domain. There, objects did not need to be called out of memory. They seemed to emerge from nowhere and lay themselves at her feet like so many delightful offerings, rich with promise and suggestion, perhaps because she sought nothing in particular, and had no idea of what she might stumble upon. But such was not the case today, since she had set out on her mission with a clear goal. Still, that goal did not keep her from reflecting upon the trivial mementos that were wont to call up the shade of the Rear-Admiral and, through their spell, bring the glorious history of the McEvoys once more to life.

She began by squatting in front of her father's old sea chest. Its wood was worm-eaten, its bronze ornamental hinges dented. The initials in gold leaf that had once stood out against the blue Moroccan leather finish had long ago become illegible. Still, its lock had not been entirely consumed by rust, and it yielded at the touch of Lily's finger. The domed cover lifted in a single movement. The chest was full to overflowing. From it rushed a cascade of moth-eaten blankets, which nearly carried with them a tea box that had been placed atop the pile. Lily caught it in the nick of time. This box had once contained several handfuls of the Rear-Admiral's home soil. But the cover was not airtight, and over the years it allowed the air to penetrate. Now only dust remained. Yet it was the apple of Lily's eye.

Rear-Admiral Magnus McEvoy was the scion of an old Irish family from the north of County Armagh, in Ulster, not far from Emain Macha, the legendary seat of King Conchobar. In 1692, in the wake of the Orange victory, grandfather McEvoy's title of magistrate had been revoked under the penal laws enacted against the Catholics. His father, who had dreamed of a career as an officer, had to settle for a life of managing the estate of an absentee landlord. Wishing to spare his only son such indignity, he had him reared in the Protestant religion and sent him off to apprentice in the Plymouth naval yards. When he was ten, Magnus put out to sea, and spent his youth coasting the Baltic ports. His special aptitude for navigation was apparent by the time he joined the Royal Navy. The first test of his talents as a pilot came against the French, in the Bay of Biscay, and off Cape Finisterre in 1747. Appointed second master of a brig at the beginning of the Seven Years' War, he replaced his grievously wounded captain during a skirmish off Cabo de Gata. There, through a series of skillful maneuvers, he drove a sixty-gun French frigate, *La Galante*, onto the shoals. He was rewarded with the captainship of the captured vessel, which he re-christened the *Galatea*, in honor of its female figurehead that seemed so alive to him that she might speak at any minute. He was only thirty years old at the time.

The sextant, compass and navigator's calipers presented to him by the admiralty on that occasion were stowed in a compartment of the chest, their brass boxes proudly engraved with his name. Yet Lily's hand chose to pass them over, and came to rest on the Rear-Admiral's cat-o'-nine-tails, a horn-handled whip whose tanned leather lashes were treated with birch oil, and whose knotted extremities were still flecked with dried blood.

When it came to cruelty, Magnus McEvoy enjoyed no better nor no worse a reputation than his fellow officers of the British fleet. He himself would punish the crew members who refused to obey his orders. Those who fell asleep on watch or indulged in impure acts would be forced to run the gauntlet between two lines of sailors who lashed them with birches. But no matter how grievous their faults, he would never deprive them of their ration of rum. In truth, his weakest point was his excessive language. His obscenities would sometimes exceed the understanding of even the most sea-hardened sailors.

In the spring of 1759, when Wolfe sailed off in conquest of Quebec, the *Galatea* was assigned to protect the convoy of eight thousand, five hundred men. In the course of the Atlantic crossing, the young captain had an excellent opportunity to distinguish himself, giving chase to *L'Insolent*, a second-class French vessel encountered off Newfoundland, which preferred scuttling to capture. Admiral Saunders, impressed by Magnus McEvoy's audacity, appointed him commander of the lead squadron, which was given the task of clearing the passage to the Île d'Orléans. By June 26, not a hostile vessel was to be found in the Saint Lawrence estuary, and Wolfe's troops were able to disembark unimpeded at Beaumont. Following the victory, Magnus McEvoy was granted permission to assist Captain James Cook in his hydrographic survey of the river. Those two months spent determining the varying depths of the water and computing the strength of currents and tides were to remain among his fondest memories of the war.

One of the maps he had drawn in the course of those happy expeditions lay flattened at the bottom of the chest. With an adroit flick of the wrist, Lily grasped the roll between her first two fingers, then spread it on the attic floor, taking pains not to tear the parchment. With great feeling, she recognized her father's hand in the angular lines illustrating the twists, turns and windings of the underwater currents that undulated through the section of the river separating Cap Saint-Ignace from Cap Diamant. Nostalgia filled her, but it was nothing compared to her shock when she perceived, at the exact center of the map, a heavy line of blue ink that divided the waters into two.

The Rear-Admiral had shown Lily this very line of demarcation on her ninth birthday. He had awakened her before sunrise and placed her, still drowsy, in the back of the carriage. Of the journey itself Lily could remember only the wisps of fog that lined the roadway, and the snorting of the horses in front of them. They may have stopped along the way, but Lily thought not. Most probably her father had turned to her, at one point or another, to give her a lump of cheese or an oatmeal cake from his pouch, cautioning her with a wink to leave no crumbs on the seat.

By noon they reached the St. Lawrence River. Taking his daughter by the hand, the Rear-Admiral helped her jump from the carriage, over the step, and led her to the water's edge. The shoreline was a broad expanse of gray mud into which one's feet sunk rapidly. Lily, who did not wish to soil her shoes, leaped from one slate shoal to another without losing her balance, delighted at the pop of the bladder-shaped fucus buds and the crackle of the fragile periwinkle shells beneath her soles. Yellow with scum, those waves that reached the shore seemed to come from an island that appeared to float in the molten tin of the river. Lily could not remember whether her father had spoken its name or not. According to the map, it could be none other than Grosse Île.

The Rear-Admiral bent down to scrutinize the algae that clung to the rocks. Then he wetted his fingers in the river water and three times brought them to his tongue. Finally, lifting Lily with one arm while she clung to his neck, he stretched out his free hand and drew an imaginary dividing line. "This is the place where fresh water ends, and salt water begins." In Lily's eyes, her father accomplished a miracle as astonishing as the parting of the Red Sea. She had done as he did, dipping her fingers into two swells of the river. "The salt water is sweeter," she exclaimed to her father's great amusement. Yes, she was indeed a McEvoy. Blood will out; her veins ran with sea water. On the day of her baptism, had she not cooed with delight when Father Compain placed a pinch of holy salt on her tongue, swaying her to and fro as though she was being rocked by the swell? But when the lustral water had been poured over her head, only a second pinch of salt could calm her cries.

After the episode of the dividing of the waters, the Rear-Admiral undertook to educate her, affectionately nicknaming her "my little river nymph." Seizing every occasion to further her instruction, he would take her in tow wherever he went, even into the meadows where he would deposit, prior to the autumn hunting season, loaves of salted clay to attract deer. In May, when the contracts to supply the governor's residence and the diocese would be negotiated, Lily would accompany her father to Quebec City. On one such trip, she was granted, at her tender age, an audience with Baron Dorchester, and Monsignor Briand in his private apartments.

Every year, she watched as the Rear-Admiral bargained for a higher price, arguing an unexpected shortage of salt, all the while distributing his precious merchandise parsimoniously, the better to keep the price high. His distinguished customers loosened their purse strings with no concern for their outlay. To bargain would have been futile. Rear-Admiral McEvoy owned the sole rock-salt mine in the land, and enjoyed an absolute monopoly. To accuse him of thievery would have entailed the risk of losing one's supplies for an entire year. Like the rest of the populace they could, of course, always fall back on imported salt from the West Indies, harvested from the marshes of Tortuga, Anguilla and the Greater Turks. But that salt, transported deep in ships' holds alongside casks of molasses or rum, was gray and bitter, good only for preserving the eels that river fishermen would catch by the thousands at the mouths of its tributaries. No, truly, it would have been inconceivable for the prelate, let alone the magistrate, to sit down at table without the incomparable salt of Armagh.

Of a diamond whiteness that admitted no impurity, the substance extracted from the McEvoy mine was unctuous to the touch, and soft enough to be ground to a powder finer than perfumed talc. Its flavor, at once strange and familiar, was so intense that the slightest soupçon was enough to season a dish. No need for pepper, cloves, cinnamon or ginger with this salt at hand. It could transform the most Spartan dish into a delicacy, and was celebrated for restoring appetite to those who had lost it. Each grain had an almost surreptitious way of clinging to the taste buds, depositing there its indissoluble imprint. Once one had tasted it, it became impossible to do without. Still, if abused, it would go to the head like sparkling wine.

The very thought of Armagh salt made Lily feel indisposed. Just as had happened earlier, in the kitchen, a feeling of light-headedness brought beads of perspiration to her forehead. Overhead, the inverted ship's hold of the roof began to turn counter-clockwise and, beneath her feet, the floorboards swayed as though they would never stop. Hands moist and stomach roiling, Lily felt on the verge of fainting dead away. She knew the symptoms far too well to mistake them with mere "vapors." Quickly, she withdrew a slender amethyst vial from her purse and removed its cap. With a trembling hand, she brought the vial close to her face and sniffed the white powder it contained. Her nostrils reacted with a flutter, warding off a sneeze. She took a long, deep breath, then exhaled in relief. Her body relaxed; she opened her eyes. The fruit of the Armagh mine revived her far better than any smelling salts could ever have.

The vial, which she kept on her person at all times, had belonged to Monsignor Briand. He had given it to Lily upon her first visit to the diocese. She would recall that adventure whenever her affliction returned to torment her. Now, she needed that memory once more.

She and her father had arrived early that morning in Quebec City, so early in fact that the bishop was unprepared to receive them. The secretary of the diocese, a pot-bellied canon whose cheeks glowed with good health, led them into the parlor of the seminary, where one of the curates was patiently reading his breviary. Being well acquainted with the Rear-Admiral, as the two men had met many times before, he began the conversation with an exchange of commonplaces before bringing up the subject of deepest concern to him: how had the salt harvest been this year, and to how many pounds was each member of the clergy entitled?

After the inactivity of the journey, Lily could hold still no longer. When her father had his back turned, she slipped away to stretch her legs. She wandered down a deserted hallway, its polished wood paneling interspersed with recesses in which tapers were burning beneath the soot-stained portraits of Monsignors Laval, Saint-Vallier, Duplessis de Mornay, Dosquet, Lauberivière and Dubreuil de Pontbriand. She made her way past a succession of closed doors, and came to a stop before one that was half open. She pushed it, and so entered an immense room whose hardwood floor was covered with carpets. There, alone at the far end of a massive table, Monsignor Briand was about to begin his breakfast.

The bishop, who was to officiate that day at the feast of Saint Ubald, was in his ecclesiastical finery, with a crucifix atop his chest and his purple hose. His crosier, his miter and his embroidered gloves lay on a chair behind him.

Judging from the pallid gray of his complexion and the circles under his eyes, it was clear that his health had already begun to suffer from the strange malady that was to force his resignation six months later. Yet he had not lost his sense of dignity. No sooner did he notice Lily than he beckoned her to draw near, and extended his right hand for her to kiss. On his third finger he wore a gold ring in which was set an amethyst that would have been heavier to bear than a cross, judging from the softness of his fingers—a softness that was all the more apparent since they were entirely without nails. How had he lost them? Had they been pulled out by the Iroquois during a missionary expedition, or had he chewed them to the quick? He gave Lily no opportunity to ask. Forcing a smile that was intended

28

to be benevolent, he invited her to sit down at the table. In front of her he placed a pitcher of double cream, a basket of hot bread and a pyramid of oranges fresh off the ship, whose pungent odor pervaded the room. He claimed for himself the single soft-boiled egg, which he peeled and abundantly salted before reciting the benediction. No sooner had he completed the prayer than he attacked it with the voracity of old age, adding a fresh dusting of salt after each mouthful. His cheeks worked with the agility of a crustacean's mouthparts. The yolk ran in filaments down his ill-shaven, blue-mottled chin. Twice he threw back his head, better to enjoy the taste. Finally, he turned his attention to Lily who had been observing him, eyes wide with fascination.

"So, you're Magnus McEvoy's daughter, are you?" he had said in an almost accusing tone. "Have you reached the age of reason?"

"Yes Monsignor."

"Have you been instructed in the principal truths of religion?"

"I know my catechism by heart."

"Tell me then, what is salt?"

He looked at her as would a cat upon a freshly captured mouse. He may have thought he could confound her with the question, but he was mistaken. Lily, swaying back and forth on her chair, tossed her red hair and answered defiantly.

"The sign of wisdom and the taste of the things of heaven."

"And why do we add it to holy water?" Monsignor Briand pursued, crushing the eggshell between his fingers.

"To preserve our souls from corruption and protect them against the Devil."

"Are you afraid of the Devil?"

"Very afraid, Monsignor, and of Hell as well."

"And what must you do to avoid the burning waste of flame and sulfur?"

"I must take care always to eat salty food."

Upon those words, the bishop raised his hand and assumed an incensed air.

"Poor child! Do you know how many Christians have eaten salt all their lives, yet have been damned for eternity?"

For a moment he was absorbed in the contemplation of his amethyst, struck by a ray of light that had strayed through the window. When he spoke once more, he was perfectly calm. It was as though he were chanting.

"*Vos estis sal terrae quod si sal evanuerit in quo sallietur ad nihilum valet ultra nisi ut mittatur foras et conculcetur ab hominus* ... Do you know those words?"

"I never learned Latin."

"It is from the Gospel According to Saint Matthew. 'You are the salt of the earth. But if the salt lose its savor, wherewith shall it be salted? It is good for nothing anymore but to be cast out, and to be trodden on by men.' So little is needed to close the gates of heaven to us—a single mortal sin, a single pernicious lie. Do not forget that when you answer the question I am going to ask you: how deep is the Armagh mine?"

"Even if I told you the truth, Monsignor, you would not believe me."

"It is not I, but God, who will judge you."

To this very day, Lily preferred to believe that she had resisted Monsignor Briand's assaults, and stood fast in the face of his threats, rather than break the seal of silence entrusted to her by her father. In reality, it had taken precious little inducement for her to reveal that seven ladders led downward to the floor of the mine, and that it could be illuminated by a single torch, so brightly did the salt crystals reflect the light. She gave a detailed description of the main chamber, where the human voice would be lost in echo upon echo; of its vaulted ceiling, which loomed higher than the new Quebec cathedral; of its thirty pillars among which one could lose one's way as in the deepest forest. She also gave the bishop a detailed account of the fifteen Indian slaves who toiled fifty feet below the ground. They were of the Pawnee nation, and had been brought from the banks of the Missouri. The Rear-Admiral had purchased them at auction, at the Seigneur of Longueuil's, for a price of forty shillings each. They had Christian names, having been duly baptized, and understood English though they obstinately refused to speak it. To prevent their escape, the Rear-Admiral made them sleep in the mine, allowing them outside only once a month, and then with shackled feet. The rest of the time they spent breaking blocks of salt from the walls, cutting them and loading them into wicker baskets, to be lifted to the surface by a system of pulleys whose ropes were pulled by four blind horses.

Lily was about to enlarge on her descriptions when suddenly she stopped. She did not feel well. The room was too warm, and worse, the cloying smell of oranges had unsettled her stomach. The bishop, ascribing her hesitation to thirst, offered her a goblet of wine cut with water, a smile of ineffable sweetness on his face, and urged her to drink. She refused, he insisted, and his sudden solicitude awoke in her a troubling mistrust. It occurred to her that the old man, having gotten from her what he was interested in, now intended to poison her.

The danger was great, but almost negligible compared to what would transpire if Monsignor Briand suspected she had guessed his sinister intentions. His true face would then appear, and who could tell what was hidden behind his mask of civility? Lily would rather die than discover that truth. Docilely, she accepted the goblet from the bishop's outstretched hand and downed it in one gulp without betraying, by either a trembling hand or a whimper, her expectation of being struck down then and there. Suddenly, the cathedral chimes struck seven times, as if they were tolling for her. It was too late to flee; her body would no longer carry her. She barely had time to see the black shapes fill the room before plummeting into darkness.

She did not remember closing her eyes. But when she reopened them, it was daylight once again. Her head was lying atop the table amid the scattered oranges. The goblet had rolled further off, beyond the eggshells. Monsignor Briand was standing behind her and moving something beneath her nose, instructing her to breathe. At first Lily was sure he was preparing to finish her off. Yet she quickly changed her mind. Fearing the bishop no more, realizing she had sorely misjudged him, she allowed herself to be revived. For she had recognized, between his spatula-like fingers, the inimitable fragrance of Armagh salt.

"It is nothing," said the bishop. "Just a swoon. It often happens to me. Fortunately, I have here the best remedy."

After helping her to sit up, he showed her the vial of salt that had been fashioned, according to his instructions, by a skilled craftsman from Beaumont named Anselm. The belly of the vial, an amethyst decorated with a pretty relief representing the Quebec cathedral, was no larger than Lily's hand. Its neck, slightly flared, was sealed with a multi-faceted stopper. Monsignor Briand had sunk a small fortune into that vial. In addition to paying Master Anselm for his work, he had provided the amethyst himself. A trifle, really, considering that Armagh salt, when taken in like fashion, possessed curative and preservative properties that made it worth its weight in gold. You need only know the ritual, explained the bishop, who soon instructed Lily how to sprinkle a few grains of salt on the back of her hand, wasting nothing, and, after shaping it into a tiny pile, how to inhale it without sneezing.

There they sat, the elderly man and the child, sniffing each in turn, contented looks on their faces, until the bishop's secretary interrupted to announce that audiences were about to begin. Before Lily could make her exit, Monsignor Briand held her back by her sleeve.

"The vial is yours," he whispered, "if you tell me one last thing. How many tonnes of salt do your father's reserves contain?"

In truth, Lily did not know the answer, and had no way of knowing. The Rear-Admiral jealously withheld the secret even from her, for it would have been the true index of the rarity of Armagh salt and, consequently, of the price he could hope to command. So eager was she to own the vial, she did not bother with such minor details. Having sworn upon the cross as Monsignor Briand demanded of her, she uttered the first figure to spring to mind. The bishop seemed surprised, though whether his surprise was one of relief or disappointment, Lily could not say.

A single pernicious lie. A single mortal sin. And so it was that, for a vial of salt, she denied herself Heaven.

Lily's memory of her encounter with the bishop was vivid—so vivid that it was clearer than more recent events. The same was true of everything that touched her use of the vial. The light, the textures, the sounds in which she luxuriated in those moments of weakness illuminated in her memory stigmata so compelling that even the wearying effect of time could not extinguish them. She was certain of one thing. With all due respect to Monsignor Briand's opinion, Armagh salt was far more than a condiment or a remedy against fainting. It was a magic powder that made it possible to capture and conserve fleeting visions, passing sensations, ephemeral happiness—all that, in life, is doomed to vanish in a cloud of smoke. Lily turned to her vial every time she feared forgetfulness. She now believed, rightly or wrongly, that she could seek out the traces of her past, as far back as their most ancient origins.

As with any sustained practice, the salt ritual was accompanied by discipline and the proliferation of rules of conduct. The first of them provided for the elimination of sweet dishes, which she considered as harmful as lotus, for with a single spoonful the reminiscences of an entire day could be eradicated. Then came exercises in purification through frequent saline ablutions and the sacrifice of all ornaments, which were exiled to the attic. There was the obligation to keep the drapes drawn; the imposition, alongside the other forms of penitence, of lengthy periods of silence; and finally, the daily offering of tears, the precious salt of the soul, which she would harvest in crystal cupels once they had evaporated.

Lily's tears had once flowed in abundance, but lately they were more difficult to obtain. Her eyes were too dry. Though she bathed them every four hours, each time she closed her eyelids she felt a burning sensation that would be horribly exacerbated by the slightest particle of dust. Which is why Perpetuity had been ordered to extirpate any such worrisome particles from the house.

In the attic, where the rope ladder stood as a boundary beyond which the maidservant could not pass, and where no feather duster ever ventured, Lily began to feel the effects. Not only her eyes, but her entire body seemed to be withering in aridity—her fingertips cracked until they bled, her lips peeled like a birch tree shedding its bark, the skin of her back was stretched taut. Yet Lily never considered drinking, afraid that a measure of sweet water would dilute the concentration of memory she so desired. And so many facets of her history remained to be illuminated before Master Anselm's arrival …

Such as the day she had passed through the village of Beaumont. Lily would have been almost fifteen at the time. Titus, who would have been seventeen, was driving the carriage for the first time. The Rear-Admiral had already begun to suffer from gout, and was too indisposed to hold the reins himself. He ordered the farmhand to accompany them to Quebec City.

The weather was cold and windy, and negotiations with Monsignor d'Esgly had been extraordinarily arduous, none of which improved the mine owner's mood. Lily's disclosures to his predecessor several years earlier had, it appears, reached the bishop's ears. Magnus McEvoy's explanation of the recent salt shortage at Armagh had been received with an incredulity that admitted of no new price increase.

The Rear-Admiral, exhausted by having to make concessions for which he had been ill-prepared, fell asleep in the carriage as they made their way back to the estate. Titus had been instructed to circumvent Beaumont by taking the road that followed the shore. But while his master slept, he took the short-cut through the village. Lily let him go without a word. If the heedless lad wished to expose himself to a torrent of curses should the Rear-Admiral awake to find himself in the place in which he had always refused to set foot, so much the worse for the boy. Meanwhile, she intended to use the opportunity to see with her own eyes this forbidden place that inspired in her such curiosity mainly because, question as she might, she never could elucidate the reasons for which her father held Beaumont in such aversion.

Though Lily had no particular idea of what might have awaited her, the village was a disappointment. Despite its mill, church and bridge, it was nothing more than a hamlet with a few primitive whitewashed farmhouses and, further along, a handful of workshops, one of whose shutters were battened, making it impossible to determine whether it was a carder's or a smithy's. The horses, which had slowed their pace when they drew near Beaumont, passed through the town in the twinkling of an eye, encountering not a single living soul.

The cemetery was not far behind them when Titus brought the gig to a stop in front of a processional chapel built along the roadside. Its once-slender silhouette had been truncated after the loss of its steeple in a violent thunderstorm.

"Why are you stopping here?" asked Lily when she saw the farmhand hitching the horses to a tree.

He motioned to her to follow him and not make a sound. First making sure that her father was still sound asleep, Lily set out after him.

The chapel was barely larger than the salt room at Armagh, and as illuminated as the latter was dark. The sun's rays shone through the hole left in the roof by the fallen steeple, and after spreading over the walls, converged upon the altar. The sculpted altarpiece must have been an object of particular devotion, for several copious bouquets of daisies had been left at its base. It was a bas-relief, carved into a single sheet of slate, that presented the faithful with the consoling image of Our Lady of the River walking upon the water. Behind her, in an ingenious display of layering that created an illusion of depth, frigates could be made out against the cliffs of Cap Diamant, with Quebec City barely visible in the distance.

Lily hastily crossed herself, clambered over the balustrade and stepped up to the altar, the better to examine the depiction of Our Lady, whose erect head and prominent bust reminded her of her mother in her moments of absence. Shells festooned her neck and algae entwined her hair. The fur cloak that draped her shoulders cascaded to her webbed feet, which were pitilessly crushing an eel.

"The man who carved this altarpiece comes from Beaumont," Titus declared. "His name is Master Anselm."

Lily gave a start of surprise. She knew the name well. She first heard it from the mouth of Monsignor Briand when he showed her his amethyst vial, and then from Father Compain each time he brought the Rear-Admiral a new salt shaker for his collection, "with compliments of Master Anselm." The salt shakers were carved from the hardest stones, worked in bas-relief and represented celebrated sailing vessels. Her father, upon receiving them, would lock them away without a word in the dining room sideboard, from which they would never emerge.

"Are you sure?" Lily asked.

"Father Compain told me so himself, when he brought me here for prayers."

Titus pointed out the delicacy with which the artisan's stylus had reproduced the votive statue's garments, particularly the striated texture of the fur. The work of the mysterious Anselm was nothing new to Lily, but the farmhand's reactions were.

Titus had changed considerably of late. Ursula and Perpetuity opined, not without justification, that he had grown like a weed, and Lily could not help but notice, as he stood next to her, that he now towered a good head above her. His face had taken on an expression of assurance as his features became better defined. A smile flickered in the corners of his eyes, which seemed to mock her each time he caught a glimpse of her. The more familiar Titus became with Lily, the more she felt she needed to escape him. Yet she would spend her days secretly observing his comings and goings, and could not endure to be out of sight of him. Often she would seek him out in the barn, where she stood like a pillar as he threshed the grain with his flail—all the while keeping close to the door, ready to escape should he attempt to approach her.

She had taken no such precautions in the chapel. And so Titus was able to corner her. Now he was advancing toward her, as purposeful as a noose closing its slipknot. His sleeves were rolled up, showing two veins that protruded disturbingly from his arms, swollen, as it were, with ulterior motives.

He covered the distance between them just as Lily had least expected it. Grasping her by the waist, he lifted her up and deposited her atop the altar. Too startled to protest, too startled even to cry out, she found herself struggling to keep her balance atop the narrow table.

"Stretch out your arms, lift your head and don't move," he told her, sizing her up with his eyes.

She had no intention of obeying his command. But she felt constrained to do so as the burning blush of confusion crept across her cheeks. Quickly she turned her head toward the opening through which the bluish glow of the sky and the salty mist of the St. Lawrence filtered into the chapel, not quite reaching her. Had it not been for the brightness, Lily could have imagined herself in the mineshaft, at that exact spot where, viewed from the surface, the rope ladder descending into the earth disappeared to join the darkness. The same stony echo, the same salt-charged drafts. Into Lily's mind sprung the hidden connections that seemed to join Beaumont and Armagh, her father and Master Anselm ... Titus, unfortunately, intruded on her reverie.

"You are more beautiful than Our Lady of the River," he told her. "You have the profile of a statue."

There was no trace of irony in his voice, yet she was sure he was making sport of her. All the more so when he clasped her knees in his sinewy arms. She became indignant; he protested his innocence. How could she doubt he had any other intention than to help her down from the altar? She had been naive enough to trust him. She had let herself drift toward him, abandoning herself like a ship sinking beneath the waves, indifferent to the rustling of her skirts about her thighs. Once her feet were on the ground, she could not break free. Titus was hugging her so tightly that through the fabric of her corset she could feel his insistent veins throbbing against her, like a knocker hammering on a closed door.

The last time he had held her so, they were children, playing in the orchard. A thunderstorm had broken, and they climbed into the wild cherry tree in search of shelter. Eaten away by dry rot, one of the tree's branches snapped beneath their feet. Lily scarcely had time to realize what had happened when Titus, like a falcon striking its prey, swept her body to his with one arm, clutching fast the trunk with the other. They remained suspended in mid-air, trembling in the embrace, unable to find their footing without falling to the ground below. Finally the Rear-Admiral, hearing their cries, rushed to their rescue. He first delivered Lily then, seeing she was more scared than hurt, turned his rage upon Titus. That the scamp had put his daughter in danger was itself an act deserving chastisement. That he had left the barn when the Rear-Admiral had expressly forbidden him to do so warranted more than the whip. He seized him by the collar, dragged him to the manure pit and thrust the lad's head into it, whipping his back with a curry-comb until the blood flowed. Titus remembered the punishment long afterward, but its effects, judging by his newfound temerity, had worn off.

To Lily it seemed as though he had dragged her to the edge of a bottomless precipice. To avoid falling, she had no choice but to hold fast to him. If her father were to awake and discover them in that frozen embrace, she was certain he would hang Titus then and there, without any form of trial. She strained to hear his approach, but there was nothing outside but silence. Inside, Titus's breathing seemed to contain a multitude of voices.

"Leave me be," she whimpered. "You're cutting off my circulation."

He did not insist. He pushed her away with these words.

"One day, I will leave. I will come here, to Beaumont, and I will make statues."

So unlikely did the idea seem to her that she stopped still on the chapel threshold and laughed.

"I will never allow it. You will always be the valet at Armagh, and you will always serve me."

In the depths of slumber in his carriage, the Rear-Admiral did not open his eyes until the manor came into view. He knew nothing of the drive through Beaumont and the lengthy stopover at the chapel. Though his providential sleep saved Titus from punishment, it simply preserved the boy for the far more dreadful chastisement that awaited him, through which Lily's prediction would come true. Surely she would have been tempted to draw some satisfaction from it, had not fate proved her so cruelly right, and if her part in the appalling incident that was to crush Titus's hopes forever had not at times filled her with remorse. She had been but an innocent onlooker. She had acted thoughtlessly, in ignorance of her father's deeply rooted spite and with little understanding of his maniacal temperament.

All this she must dismiss from her mind. It was still too early to think about it. Some memories were reserved for Master Anselm, and would have to await the supper hour.

Outside the attic, the great hustle and bustle of the spring morning was already underway. At Armagh, the wind blew more fiercely than elsewhere in the township. Sometimes it was so heavily laden with salt that it seemed to come from the ocean, and not the environs of the mine. Now it set the aspen branches creaking like ill-oiled hinges. The birds quarreled among themselves with choruses of mind-numbing chirps, while the bees contrived to throw the compartments of this immense hive into a commotion. The attic, though, was far removed from the confusion. It had its own slow order, measured by the deep breathing of its occupants as they slumbered. Chiffoniers and writing desks, dressing tables and flowerpots, drums, picture frames, blotters, ottomans and night lanterns, wing chairs and scent boxes lay peaceably at rest, lodged tightly one against the other. All of them but the Rear-Admiral's pistol, which glistened in its case.

Lily knew the pistol well. It had been part of her father's booty from *La Galante*. Its marbled brass patch-box was engraved with the signature of the Frères Roy, the celebrated gunsmiths of La Rochelle. Its walnut stock, carved with floral patterns and escutcheons, ended in a pommel that represented a dogfish. The trigger guard and the ramrod eyelets were of solid silver, and the breech plug of steel. Five pans in diameter, its barrel displayed a cannon mouth, customary in naval practice, from which had issued, one day as Lily was shooting ravens for practice, a cloud of smoke in the form of a human hand.

Lily was seventeen at the time, and had just lost her mother. Mourning may have made her vulnerable to illusion, for she swore she saw the smoky hand grasp at the air, feel about in empty space as if seeking direction. Her initial curiosity turned to terror when the black fingers turned toward her and began to creep up the pistol barrel in a series of convulsions. Had Lily succumbed to instinct, she would have thrown the pistol into the grass and leaped over the fence to put herself out of reach. But she steeled herself and, obeying a sudden surge of vindictiveness, squeezed the trigger. The threatening hand, swept away by the shot, had just enough time to assume the shape of a fist before being dispersed by the wind.

Brandishing the pistol at arm's length like a triumphal banner, Lily returned to the manor by the shortest path, the one the cattle used. As she passed in front of the barn, she paused on the threshold and hazarded a glance inside. Her hope was to catch Titus unawares behind the sacks of oats where, every evening, he stowed his pitchforks. Two years had elapsed since their escapade at Beaumont, and since then the valet had become secretive, emerging on rare occasions from the farm buildings and his mute state. He had a secret and Lily, for all her extraordinary vigilance, had not yet been able to discover it.

The barn seemed deserted and still, except for a flight of rainbows whose bright patterns danced across the roof beams, the joists and the planked partitions. In the hayloft Titus, wearing a homespun shirt, his legs bare, lay on his stomach. There he held, in a ray of sunlight, a crystalline object that he hastily thrust into the hay when he heard footsteps mounting the ladder. But he was unable to completely suppress the flickering.

Lily had caught Titus in the act, but pretended she had seen nothing. She lay down beside him and related her adventure. He hefted the pistol, and examined the black powder residue that had collected at the end of the barrel before venturing an opinion: the smoky hand might well have belonged to the ghost of one of the runaway slaves whom His Excellency had hunted down last year.

"You are mistaken," Lily replied. "It can only be Beeton, the old sailor who blew up the *Galatea* when he set fire to a cask of rum."

In 1762, she told him, Magnus McEvoy had just been commissioned Rear-Admiral. His orders were to sail from Quebec and set a course for Havana, where the Blue Fleet awaited. But he got no farther than Newfoundland. There, in Placentia Bay, where the *Galatea* was forced to lay over to carry out repairs on the foreyard, a flock of ravens suddenly darkened the sky before settling onto the masts. There must have been at least four hundred of them, causing the struts to sag and damaging the rigging. The crew, who would never harm a bird for fear of incurring the wrath of Heaven, attempted to dislodge them by persuasion. The men's cries were lost amid the deafening chatter. At times the marauders would take to the air at their approach, but return to their perches once the coast was clear.

Under normal circumstances, Magnus McEvoy tried to respect the superstitions of his men. This time, circumstances left him no choice. With a rain of excreta, the ravens were threatening to engulf the vessel's very soul, the figurehead that was the Rear-Admiral's pride and joy. Drawing a bead on the largest bird, which had perched on the bowsprit like a sentinel, he cocked his pistol. Just as he was about to fire, old Beeton the quartermaster thrust himself in front of him in an attempt to protect the raven. In the Rear-Admiral's eyes, this was a clear case of mutiny, no more and no less, and he punished the man with an extraordinary measure.

"You will be deprived of your ration of rum until you have rid the ship of these birds," he informed the quartermaster, handing him the pistol.

Beeton refused to take it. He would have preferred to die of thirst than be the bearer of malediction.

"Since that is the case," the Rear-Admiral answered, "you will be banished to the topsail yardarm amongst the ravens until they leave of their own accord."

One day passed, then a second, then a third. It was clear that the ravens nesting in the masts were not of a mind to move. After fruitless attempts, Beeton abandoned all hope of frightening them, and now sat as motionless as they, moving only at sundown when the vapors of the rum the Rear-Admiral distributed to the crew wafted upward to reach him. Eyes half closed, he opened his voracious beak and emitted a blood-curdling croak. So badly did he miss his alcohol that he began to seethe with fury against those who were drinking far below. He lashed out at his unjust punishment. Why should he be deprived of alcohol when his act of insubordination had saved the entire crew? The men, ill-given to solidarity, crossed themselves furtively when they heard his oaths of vengeance. For them, he had become nothing more than another augury of misfortune.

On the fourth day, under cover of heavy fog, Beeton made his way down to the bridge, and slipped undetected to where the cask of rum was stored. He threw a handful of gunpowder onto the cask, then lit it with the flame of a lamp. Faster than you could shout "Watch out," everything was blown sky high. Twenty-two men—but not a single raven—perished in the blast, including Beeton.

"That is how my father found himself, quite suddenly, without a ship, without a commission, and in mourning for his figure-head," Lily concluded.

In an attempt to distract her, Titus urged her to continue her story. She told how the Rear-Admiral made his way back to Quebec on the frigate that had rescued him and the remainder of his crew, three days after the signature of the Treaty of Paris. War weary, sea weary, retired on half-pension, he began making preparations to return to Ireland. It was then that the Governor General, James Murray, concerned by the meager contingent of British immigrants in the new colony, granted him, in recognition of his participation in the Conquest, irrevocable title to twenty thousand acres of virgin land extending from both banks of the Loutre River, a distance of two days on foot from the village of Beaumont.

The best way to get there was to skirt the marshes by way of the cove, and then, turning due east, to follow the forest road that crossed the Saint-Michel Arm and La Chute Creek, before traveling past the rapids at Le Sault as far as the bend in the Loutre. More than once during the journey, Magnus McEvoy wondered how he, a captain of ocean-going vessels, could possibly inhabit a land that seemed to ooze fresh water from every pore. But as he crossed the land that would be his, he came to realize that copious surface water was by no means its sole quality.

He, not his mount, discovered the salt spring when, at dusk, he stopped to rest, Lily continued. Just as the lightning flash is visible before the thunderclap, her father spied the mists wafting through the air well before he heard the babbling of the waters. He followed the sound to its source along a hillside, until he reached the mossy hollow from which the spring spilled forth in bubbling torrents from between the rocks. How greatly relieved he was when he discovered that the water was saline. He could not resist the impulse to fill his cupped hands and sprinkle the soil. Thus did he baptize his estate Armagh, in honor of his native land.

The following day, as he tried to sound the depth of the well-spring, the point of his saber struck an obstacle whose whiteness and resistance suggested glacial ice. Appearances had not deceived him. Immersing himself to the waist in the icy waters, he had only to break off a piece to understand that it was indeed solid salt.

By one of those geological miracles that took place some time between the establishment of the universal sea and its subsequent ebbing, Armagh had come to rest atop a bed of rock salt fifty feet thick. Its capacity, according to Lily, had been evaluated at twenty thousand tonnes—more than enough to ensure the family's fortunes for many a generation.

During the first two years, Magnus McEvoy assigned the majority of his newly hired laborers to clearing the roads, and had been able to exploit only the surface excrescences of the mine. But in the spring of 1765, he was ready to begin under-ground production, aided by a master miner whom he had brought expressly from Northwich, County Chester, the site of the most significant British salt mines. After a summary assess-ment, this man had determined that the salt of Armagh, infinitely purer than ordinary rock salt, did not need to be refined. It could be extracted by pick and shovel instead of by the usual process of recrystallization by dissolution and evaporation.

Picks and shovels, even wielded by fifteen brawny Pawnee slaves, were altogether too slow for the Rear-Admiral's taste. Attempting to increase the mine's output, he perfected a blast-ing technique wherein whole segments of the mineral were detached from the walls of the mine by detonating charges of powder attached to small casks of rum. Once sorted, the frag-ments thus obtained were hoisted to the surface and hauled by mule-back to a point just downstream from the rapids of the Loutre River, where Magnus McEvoy had caused a hydraulic salt crusher to be built. The mill's ten steel-tipped wooden piles, driven by a water wheel, pulverized the salt at a rate of ten blows per minute, reducing it to a powder fine enough to strain through a silken sieve.

Lily's abundance of detail was meant less to provide an answer to Titus's questions, and more to feign composure as she slowly rolled onto her side and rummaged though the hay, hoping to lay hands on the object he had hidden there.

"I've often gone for a stroll by the salt works," the hired hand admitted. "I even sneaked into the mine one day when the Rear-Admiral's back was turned."

Lily sat bolt upright, hand to her heart as it pounded with alarm.

"Don't you ever set foot in there again," she advised him in a frightened voice. "Do you know what happens to people who pry into my father's business?"

With his customary nonchalance, he laughed off her threats, the white flash of his teeth stinging Lily far more than their bite would have. It may well be true, he said, that the Rear-Admiral condemned to the mine anyone who had the misfortune of being caught on his land, be they beggars, trappers, or even those American revolutionaries who, fifteen years earlier, had attempted to invade the country. Perhaps it was also true, as Ursula and Perpetuity enjoyed telling one another, that when he opened the mine, His Excellency had also opened a gateway to Hades. Through it vanished all those who had never returned from Armagh, and were he to dig deeper still, the flames would soon blaze forth, and in the end consume the entire estate and with it, its inhabitants. But such stories no longer frightened him. Titus might once have feared Magnus McEvoy, and there indeed had been a day when he shuddered at the sound of the old man's footsteps. But he feared him no longer. He was almost twenty, he had grown strong enough to defend himself against anyone, even his master, over whom he towered by a head. If the old man were to take the lash to him, Titus would not hesitate to strike first.

"You're mad!" Lily exclaimed. "He will cast you out, and then what will you do for a living?"

"I've already told you," Titus replied. "I shall go to Beaumont and make statues."

"How will you do that? You are only good for minding the animals."

He took the insult with a smile.

"Believe what you will. In any event, I've made up my mind."

Come summer's end, he said, as soon as the last sheaths of barley had been brought in, he would pack up his belongings and leave, never to return. Why would he miss Armagh? For as far back as he could remember, he had known only cruelty and injustice here. Yes, he'd been a foundling, and the Rear-Admiral had been more than kind in rescuing him from the ravine in which he'd been abandoned by a young woman dishonored, or by the impoverished father of a family with too many mouths to feed. Titus had paid dearly for that generosity. Lodged in a corner of the stable between two heaps of manure, fed on what the dogs would leave him at the bottom of their bowls, never having known the sweetness of human company nor the warmth of the hearth, he absorbed more blows than an ageing mare, and spent hours of penitence on the roof of the barn, at the mercy of wind and weather.

But that was nothing compared with the ignorance in which the Rear-Admiral kept him throughout his childhood. Had it not been for Father Compain, he would never even have known the history of his faith! His visits to the parish hall, whose library boasted no fewer than one hundred and eighty-nine volumes, revealed to him the depths of his own brutishness and the rusticity of his manners. Since then, overwhelmed by feelings of shame, he had been driven by a desire to improve himself, so as never again to be humiliated. Under the orders of Magnus McEvoy, he cleared the fields, pulled stumps, hauled stones, removed snow from the roads. His debt had been paid. Nothing could stop him from seeking his freedom.

"You are an ingrate," Lily said. "You've forgotten all I've done for you. Did I not dry your tears when you cried?"

Titus threw her a sidelong glance.

"You did not dry them, Lily. You licked them. Just as you came every evening to lick the sweat from my brow."

"Can you hold that against me? Nothing is as salty as the humors of your body. I would even lick the blood from your wounds, if you would let me ..."

And as if to prove it, she bent over Titus's raw-skinned hands, fine, sensitive hands made for wearing gloves, and not for the disfigurement of field work. The valet recoiled with a start, but it was too late. Lily was able to run her tongue over his fingers— and she detected on them, beyond the shadow of a doubt, the inimitable taste of Armagh salt.

"What have you been doing in the mine?" she cried out. "You've been stealing salt, I know you have! Where are you hiding it?"

Titus answered her accusations with a shrug of his shoulders, which raised Lily's indignation to a fever pitch. Determined to get to the bottom of things, she pushed him backward with all her strength and parted the straw. What she saw so dazzled her that she cried out in spite.

It was a bust, cut off at shoulder level, that represented a young girl whose hair was swept back and held in place by a lily, and whose finely sculpted beveled petals refracted the light into more colors than the facets of a prism. Titus had sculpted it from a block of transparent salt, with the same knife he used to castrate chicks. He was not entirely satisfied with his work, having over-accentuated the hollows formed by his subject's collar bones. Still, he did not think this minor flaw would prevent him from winning a place as an apprentice with Master Anselm, were he to show him the bust.

"Did you make this with your own hands?" Lily stammered, her face falling.

Her initial vexation gave way to discouragement. She understood that those two dexterous hands were two rivals against which her own hands would be powerless when it came to keeping Titus at Armagh. She put on a contrite expression.

"How hatefully I have treated you," she uttered in a low voice. "Will you ever be able to forgive me?"

"Promise me only," the valet asked her, "to say nothing to your father about the stolen salt."

She kissed him on the cheek, and swore by her faith.

"You can count on me."

She could still remember the taste of Titus's hands that afternoon. That taste guided her now through the attic as, without a second thought, she went past dried-out herbaria, velveteen vests with faded embroidery, yellowed partitions, stuffed owls, perforated pots, torn aprons, boxes of rusty nails ... She stopped in the dustiest recess, where she had only ventured once before, in front of an armoire whose lock had been forced. No sooner did she throw open the doors than a cloud of mites swarmed in her face. She waved them away and found, on the shelf upon which she had left it, the otter-belly cloak that once belonged to her mother. She unwrapped the timeworn fur with her fingertips and revealed to the light of day that which, for ten years, had there lain enveloped. Picking up the salt bust with all the care of a nurse, she clutched it to her bosom.

"Come! At last your hour is nigh," she whispered through her sharp teeth.

II

MASTER ANSELM

In the lacy penumbra of the cedar grove, Titus was walking backwards. Three times, he had fallen into a bed of dry needles after tripping over exposed roots, and his elbows were bleeding. The deeper he plunged into the forest, the more he dissolved into its colorless indifference. The tree trunks slowly turned a darker hue and the leaves averted their faces from him. From the crowns of the maple trees came only the echo of his pounding heart.

To his annoyance, no one opened when he knocked on the door of the hut, and no one responded to his call as he paced back and forth outside it. The sun would soon be setting, and if he wanted to bring Master Anselm back to the manor in time for supper, he had no choice but to see if he might be in the area of the mine, the very mine he had sworn, many years ago, never to go near again. Walking backwards was a way of keeping to his vow, and avoiding any thought of the blood that had once stained the path. Were he to veer off course, salt, like a horse's bit, pulled him back.

The road was long, and he traveled it immersed in thought. His premonition had not deceived him. Lily was preparing another of her master-strokes. For weeks, clouds pregnant with thunder had been gathering over the manor, but the storm had not yet broken. What role had been assigned to Master Anselm in this latest tragedy? Titus had no idea. One thing, though, was certain: the invitation to supper, for all its impromptu appearance, could not be a simple act of hospitality ... But perhaps he was overly suspicious? Could he have been attributing to Lily intentions that were not hers? Perhaps he simply refused to admit what Ursula and Perpetuity had long claimed, that Her Excellency held a particular affection for Master Anselm, an attachment even. No longer willing to settle for her weekly assignations, she might have wished for a more attentive presence by her side.

The very idea of the stone carver sitting down at the McEvoy dinner table, with its silver table settings, beneath the illuminated candelabrum, made Titus's blood boil. He could not deny it. His animosity, though ten years old, had lost none of its bite. Yet for all that, it hung from such a slender thread: two or three muttered utterances, and one unfortunate word …

His resentment harked back to the day when the farmhand had traveled to Beaumont, bearing a letter the address of which he could not read, and which he presumed was intended for Father Compain. Having followed the winding road to the church, he knocked at the vicarage door. The curate was not home. A worker, busy trimming the lintels into which would be fitted the windows of the new parish hall, informed him that the vicar, who had studied surgery in his youth with Montcalm's personal physician and let it be widely known at the Hôtel-Dieu that he knew the secret of curing cankers, had gone off to apply a poultice to one of his patients.

The man had the look of a block of badly quarried stone. Everything about him was oversized: the forehead that rested atop a band of jet black eyebrows, the smile that cut a swathe through an even blacker beard, the shoulders, broad as a yoke, and above all the hands, in which the handle of his mallet all but vanished. The farmhand approached him with caution.

What had become of the young man of open countenance who smiled obligingly at all who crossed his path? The flame of his self-assurance seemed to have been snuffed out as by a lead candle snuffer, leaving behind it only a blackened wick crumpled back upon itself, through which escaped nothing but a wisp of acrid smoke. Crumpled in his clenched fist he carried the letter with which Lily had entrusted him, and he brandished it under the worker's nose, mumbling that he wished to deliver it personally to Father Compain.

The man took it from him and, after turning it over several times, asked Titus, "How do you know this letter is for the vicar?"

"I learned how to read," Titus maintained.

"Someone taught you badly. It says here: *To Master Anselm.*"

Startled at encountering such a sign of education in someone he supposed to be at least as ignorant as himself, Titus, for all that, was moved by the sound of the familiar name.

"Where can I find him?" he hastened to ask.

By way of answer, the man tore the letter open and, barely moving his lips, began to scan Lily's crude scribbles, first with a frown of incomprehension, then with growing interest. After lingering on the signature, he placed the letter in his belt and announced that, at the request of Her Excellency, he was to follow Titus to Armagh with no further delay.

He first stopped off at his house to collect a few tools, and from there he led the farmhand to a clapboard shack perched on the edge of the bluff where Église Creek joined the river. The ground floor was occupied by a workshop that had not, judging by its undisturbed appearance, been in recent use. Master Anselm lived upstairs in what he had previously used as the drafting room. There, before executing a floral tracery, a medallion

57

or a lion's head, he would calculate the lines along which he would carve the stone. These were secrets whose formulae he inscribed in the mysterious figures etched on his worktable. For this stone carver had not always been reduced to trimming lintels like a mere apprentice. He had once been one of the most highly reputed sculptors of bas-relief in the land.

He was a descendant, on his mother's side, of François de la Joue—the unfortunate overseer of the Saint John's Gate and the altarpiece of the Ursuline chapel, who had met an untimely death in Persia after having taken up a career as a silk importer. His father, an honest stone carver who resided in the village of Beaumont, taught him at an early age how to handle the bush hammer and the rasp. So well did he succeed that at age thirteen Anselm had apprenticed himself to the workshop of the architect Janson, on rue de la Fabrique, where he rapidly displayed a predisposition for ornamental masonry. Elevated to journeyman status two years later, he was hired to restore the façade of the Château Saint-Louis, which had been damaged by British cannon balls. While there, he also redid the mantelpieces, and his painstaking work won him a reputation for excelling in decorative relief. When Monsignor Briand began the reconstruction of the Quebec Cathedral in 1766, Anselm was given the commission to carve six alabaster baptismal stoups, ornamented with cherubim. The sculptor delivered his commission with such alacrity that the bishop resolved to take him into his service, and immediately entrusted the decoration of the baptistery to him.

Anselm once again gave complete satisfaction. With its interlacing lambs and doves, the frieze that adorned the baptismal fonts was, in the prelate's own words, the perfect representation of innocence and purity. Unfortunately, Anselm was unable to attend the blessing of the work. On the very day the ceremony was to take place, he was called away in all haste to the bedside of his father, who had been half-paralyzed by an attack of apoplexy.

Though he promised Monsignor Briand to return to Quebec City before the Feast of the Assumption, Anselm never again left Beaumont. He assumed the care of his father, a widower who had no other children, and became a stone carver, spending much of his time polishing gravestones. At the request of his former protector, who was inconsolable at having lost such a skilled artisan, he agreed to execute, on occasion, certain specific objects: an amethyst vial, a Saint Lawrence medal carved from selenite, a pair of jasper cruets, not to forget an altarpiece representing Our Lady of the River commissioned for the archiepiscopal chapel. Anselm also begun to carve, from a block of pink calcite, an incense boat, but Monsignor Briand died before he could complete it. It lay, unfinished, in a corner of the drafting room, where Titus spied it as he waited for the stone carver to complete his preparations.

How could he possibly have missed it? The fleur-de-lys carved in relief on the white-festooned hull brought to mind, with painful precision, memories of the time when his hands still possessed their dexterity. They were memories all the more painful for Titus to endure as he thought back to the lily that adorned the salt bust he had sculpted so long before. He could only conclude that each facet of his work was far the superior to those of this particular boat, none of which stood out from the background. He was about to take his leave when Master Anselm's voice startled him.

"Don't just stand there!" he heard the voice ring out. "Come here, and help me if you will."

The farmhand had retreated to the door mumbling, by way of excuse, more admiration for the boat than he truly felt. The stone carver accepted his compliments with a sneer of condescension.

"Do you know something about stone?" he asked in a mocking voice.

"I've polished pebbles," the farmhand replied.

"As you sharpen your scythe, no doubt."

"You are mistaken. I once dreamed of becoming a sculptor."

Master Anselm looked at him with the interest of the artist on the lookout for apprentices. Gazing from beneath their thick visor of black eyebrows, his eyes sized up the young man's build, the muscles of his shoulders and wrists, finally coming to rest on his hands. He had not noticed them before, and now he shook his head in disapproval.

"And you wanted to be a sculptor with fingers like those?" he asked the farmhand in an ill-tempered voice. "They look more like the paddles of a goose."

Titus was mortified, for he considered his flattened, twisted, disfigured fingers to be as grotesque, though once they had been unblemished. He was not in the habit of displaying them, and he cursed himself for having forgotten. Shoving his fists deep into his pockets, he swore never to withdraw them again.

Today, he considered his oath to have been excessive and ill-considered. Yet the habit he had adopted of keeping his fingers hidden, even when alone, had long pushed such considerations aside. It was clear that, ten years later, Master Anselm's judgment continued to determine his behavior.

Those were his thoughts as he felt the ground harden beneath his wooden clogs. Around him, the atmosphere had changed. The air was drier now, the woods were creaking, the trees seemed hunched over beneath the weight of old age. The mine entrance could not be more than a few paces away, and it was awaiting Titus.

He waited to cross the threshold before turning around. He had not brought a lamp, and he fully expected that he would have to feel his way through the darkness of the galleries. But the vestibule was lit by a glow that emerged from the depths of the mineshaft. Without hesitation, Titus stepped over the coping and began to go down the ladder.

The wooden rungs, the glistening walls, the column of frigid air that blew upward and against which he braced himself— everything reminded him of the day he had crept into the mine, intent on pilfering the block of salt. Everything, that is, but the sound of the mine itself, which had a new crystalline quality that Titus attributed to the subterranean glow.

Despite his attempt to make no noise, his entry into the mine had not gone unnoticed. No sooner had he set foot on the floor than Master Anselm loomed up before him. His build was even more imposing than it was in Titus's memory. So wide were his shoulders that they blocked not only the path, but also the view into the mine that lay behind him. The rest of him, however, had suffered such wear and tear that he seemed to be worn away. His face was crosshatched with deep wrinkles that reached to his neck. His pale lips were peeling; his corneas had a turbid appearance, as though they might flake off in places. Titus could not help but think of Lily: her transparent eyelids; her complexion that retained a few final traces of freshness doomed to evaporate; her uneven breathing; her tottering step that seemed to cast about for support, as if the young woman were afraid of falling and breaking to pieces. Had Master Anselm, he wondered, also contracted the loathsome habit of taking salt as if it were snuff, or was it the air of the mine that so transformed him? Whatever the reason, his decline had not made him any more amenable.

"I know who you are," he growled, in a voice that boomed like a pipe organ. "You are the valet. What are you doing here?"

Titus diligently conveyed Her Excellency's orders. He had one foot on the first rung of the ladder, and was about to make his way up, when Master Anselm grabbed him by the sleeve. His gaze seemed feverish.

"She is inviting me to the manor for supper?" he exclaimed.

"Those were her exact words. She made me repeat them."

The stone carver shook off the white powder that clung to his coat. Each sweep of his hand caused the hard crust of salt and sweat that clung to his skin to crack. His saliva, which tasted brinier than ever, burned his throat.

"If she is calling me in, it can only be because she intends to dismiss me."

Struggling to keep his balance, Titus pulled his arm free.

"What have you been doing here for these ten years?" he asked.

Instead of answering, Anselm held out a metal wire. From the end dangled an object that he swung like a pendulum. It had the shape of a tear wiped from the corner of an eye, or a rain-drop frozen in its fall. The farmhand did not need to touch it to know that the object was neither glass nor crystal.

The opportunity was too good to resist. Now he could turn the tables on the stone carver.

"That's nothing but salt," he shrugged.

"Yes, common salt," Anselm answered spitefully. "And I've dedicated the last ten years of my life to sculpting it."

Then he stepped aside, revealing a massive portal whose two panels were decorated with a letter carved in bas-relief. It depicted an *A* composed of two picks, and a sheet anchor. Its white, frosted appearance indicated that it too had been carved from salt.

"It is a replica of the Armagh gate," said Titus.

"Yes," Master Anselm confirmed. "The gate that was closed to me until Lily summoned me here ..."

He was about to embark upon an explanation, but thought better of it, and pulled the latch that barred the double doors.

"Follow me," he instructed the farmhand. "I have one final task to complete." Then raising his index finger, he added, "Before you enter, take off your clogs. And be careful where you put your feet."

Titus looked down. The ground had been paved with slabs of salt polished to a mirror sheen that reflected back to him, through small irregularities in the density of the raw material itself, his own discontinuous image. Because of its aberrations, it appeared all the more striking in its truth.

"Have you noticed that the slabs display no asperity at all?" said Master Anselm. "A technique I learned from my father."

The latter, he continued, had a firm rule. All minerals must be polished with their own dust—granite with granite, sandstone with sandstone, limestone with limestone. For him, no part of the process was as important as the polishing. It was the moment when the artisan erased every last trace of himself. It would never have occurred to him to sign a work, or to seek to set himself apart by a particular style or manner. He would have been horrified had anyone been able to recognize his handiwork in the stones he had carved. To polish, he liked to say, was to hasten the world's course towards eternity, for the Day of Judgment would come when the earth's last stone would turn to dust. To hasten the ravages of time was to fulfill the will of God.

This honest stone carver had learned the trade from his own father, who had been one of the master builders of the Beaumont church. His wish was for his son never to practice any other trade. No sooner could Anselm hold a chisel than his father removed him from his mother's skirts and took him to his workshop. The lad was not yet strong enough to dress the blocks of stone. But he was able to smooth them, and that was his task from dawn to dusk. Whenever he paused to rest, his father would throw a handful of gravel at him. If his work was wanting, his father would suspend him by a rope from the bluffs at Beaumont, and Anselm would have to polish their surface as the river waters licked at his calves.

"More than once," said the stone carver, "he left me hanging there all night. I was terrified that a river nymph would carry me off."

"A river nymph, Master Anselm?"

"It's clear you were born far from the water if you don't know what she is. A river nymph is a creature of the river, a daughter of the Saint-Lawrence. During the day she sleeps in the deeps, then she rises up through the silt, and she dresses herself in algae and fine slate. She does not swim, but makes her way upstream afoot. Which is why her feet are shaped like a duck's. She fancies eels, which she steals from our traps, for she cannot be bothered to hunt her own food. But what she finds most delicious are men. Should she spy one on the shore, she will approach him and work her wiles."

But the fear of river nymphs, added Master Anselm, was not enough to heal his ways.

"I would be telling a lie if I said I did not deserve my father's punishment. I was lazy, and I found working stone to be boring.

If the English had not come, I would have gone abroad, and plied another trade."

He still remembered the day when the troops of General Wolfe, who had landed at Beaumont the previous day, tried to burn down the church before moving on. Though the soldiers made three attempts, the flames damaged only the door. The stones, the very ones carved by Anselm's grandfather, had not even been blackened. The boy understood that in a world bound for perdition, the best course was to bequeath something enduring to posterity.

From that moment on, he began to work at a furious pace. But polishing and carving gravestones no longer sufficed; he dreamed that figures might emerge from them.

"You wanted to carve statues?" asked Titus.

"Not statues," Master Anselm hastened to correct him. "Bas-reliefs! What is the point of concentrating on the underside of the material, when all that counts is what's visible?"

But his father never allowed him to practice any form of ornamentation at all. He would have considered it a sin of pride, especially since, for him, any protuberance was equivalent to an obscenity. Had God considered the carving of bas-relief an honorable activity, he argued, the tablets of the Ten Commandments would have been sculpted, and not engraved.

Anselm, bound by filial duty, bided his time impatiently. The break was unavoidable, and it came with the death of his mother. When his father forbade him to erect anything other than a simple gravestone, without decoration and epitaph, the young man, incensed, made up his mind to complete his apprenticeship elsewhere.

"That was the time I left for Quebec City," concluded Master Anselm, as he opened the portal of salt.

Lily had not lied when she told Monsignor Briand that the main chamber of the Armagh mine was immense, and that thirty pillars of salt supported it. To preserve the integrity of the vaulted room, and make it unnecessary for the laborers to erect retaining walls, the extraction process had spared these pillars. It was in this giant room that the workhorses once were stabled. The poor beasts, deprived of daylight, had lost their sight. Titus remembered how he had hidden behind their feeding trough, the day he came to pilfer a piece of salt.

Both horses and troughs had long since disappeared, and the great room had been emptied when the mine was closed. Only the pillars remained, and even they no longer looked the same. Once crudely roughed out, they had been chiseled to resemble the trunks of maple, birch and wild-cherry trees, with their smooth or knobby bark, their protruding knots, their tufts of lichen, their clumps of fungus. Titus felt as though he were stepping into a grove of ancient trees encrusted with frost, whose foliage rose up in a frosty cradle through which could be seen a multitude of flowers, fruits and birds. Each step revealed a new detail of this fantastic fantasy of salt: an owl in the hollow of a tree trunk, a squirrel scurrying upward, a bunch of acorns ... Not an inch of the chamber had eluded the stone carver's chisel. And all of it glittered in the flickering torchlight like diamonds.

"You see," Master Anselm told Titus, "I do not share my father's taste for sobriety. My natural inclination drives me toward a profusion of motifs, a richness of textures, an excess of decorative elements. Nothing is sadder, in my view, than a surface upon which a relief has not been carved. And, in any event, what is ornamentation but the first sign of civilization?"

In Quebec City, in the various workshops and numerous sites where he had toiled, Master Anselm acquired his mastery of the wreath, foliation, and the garland. When he returned to Beaumont after his father's illness, he had been so naive as to believe he could inculcate a sense of refinement in the local peasants. But his every attempt to spread beauty encountered the incomprehension of his countrymen.

"Of course, my father expected I would do things in the traditional manner. How many times did we clash! What power did he wield over me by then? He was bedridden, unable to get up. 'You shall see,' he warned me, 'people hereabouts have no need of the frivolous.' He was right."

Master Anselm found the inhabitants of the township steeped in humility, afraid to raise themselves even to the smallest degree above their modest condition. They preferred to linger in their state of abject rusticity. Above all, for fear that their neighbors would look upon them as arrogant, they did not want to provoke jealousy. They asked nothing more of their millstones, of their well copings, of their mantelpieces than to be utilitarian, and not deviate from their function. They would grow angry if the stone carver suggested they add a decorative mask or an arabesque above their thresholds. He could not even convince them to carve a date upon the façade of their houses. Their lack of imagination threw him into consternation. He could not understand their reticence to embellish. Yet he finally accepted the mediocrity of Beaumont.

"Did you ever regret leaving Quebec City?" Titus asked him.

"Regrets, remorse ... Nothing is more useless, especially when everyone knows that things cannot be changed. I never look back, for what is behind me no longer exists. Except here. There is something about this mine, in the salt itself, which drives me, time and time again, back into my memories."

To illustrate to the farmhand exactly what he meant, he led him to the center of the chamber, into a kind of clearing where an urn of salt stood. Its relief represented a young lady caught by the rain. Water streamed from her cloak, and wet hair clung to her temples.

"This is Lily's mother," said Master Anselm, "just as she appeared before me one November night, in 1768."

Autumn had come early that year, he recalled as he caught his breath. The wind had long since stripped the trees of their leaves. Each day brought rain to Beaumont, and what rain it was! When clouds filled the sky, it grew so dark that it was impossible to get anything done in the workshop. Anselm would adjourn to the house next door, where he would look after his invalid father. Huddled close to the fire that he lacked the strength to feed, the old man barely noticed his son's presence as he stared at the hearth, riven by fits of anxiety that caused him to jump every time the shutters clattered in the wind.

One evening, when he seemed even more nervous than usual, he sent Anselm to check whether the door was properly closed. When he opened it, the young man felt something cold and damp rub against his leg. It was as if an animal had snuck past him into the house. He whirled about, prepared to chase it out.

At first he saw nothing more than a sealskin dripping on the floor. Lifting one of its folds, he discovered a young girl wetter than a strand of seaweed. Anselm drew close to her with his candle. Her eyes were the color of slate, her cheeks pale, her long hair disheveled.

"It's a river nymph!" his father cried out. "Don't let her in!"

Absorbed by the exquisitely modeled profile of the young girl, the ribbon-like strands of her hair and the harmonious folds of her garments, Anselm felt as though he were contemplating some figure escaped from an ancient bas-relief.

"Who are you?" he asked, at the risk of frightening her away. "How did you get here?"

"Can I warm myself a bit before telling you my story?" she asked.

Her voice put Anselm's teeth on edge. It sounded as though it was full of sand.

"This river nymph will not bewitch me," he said to himself. "I shall be the one to tame her."

Her name was Laurence, and she was an orphan. Her father, the youngest son of a seigneur whom she did not want to name, had been brought up in piety, but evil readings transformed him into a free thinker. Even a marriage of reason and four children could not bring him back to the straight and narrow. It had been years since he last attended Mass, or confessed. He neglected his prayers and mocked the curate. Finally, he was cast out of his father's house after having blasphemed once too often. His only worldly goods were a horse and a cart. As he knew how to play the fiddle, he traveled from barn to barn where people would dance the rigadoon. Along with him he dragged his wife and off-spring. They would sleep in the hay, feed upon crumbs, dress in rags. Freedom, he would say, lay just over the horizon. A man had to keep moving towards it.

One day he decided to explore one of the islands of the estuary. He crowded his family into a rowboat rented from a porpoise hunter, and though he had no experience as a navigator, he took to the river. Not far from the shores of the island, the waters suddenly became rough. The boat capsized and quickly sunk. Only Laurence survived the shipwreck by clinging to a reef. At high water, she floated onto the tidal mud flats. She crawled for hours through the salt marches, and was finally rescued by a widow who cared for her and nursed her back to health.

The girl stopped to sweep the cinders from the hearth and blow on the embers. She placed logs on the fire, and set the kettle to boil. At her request, Anselm plucked a sprig of wild carrot that hung drying from the ceiling in order to prepare an infusion. The old man, moping where he sat, pushed away the cup when she handed it to him.

"Don't try to poison me with your river-nymph potions," he warned her. "I'm not quite ready to step into my grave."

Undeterred, she handed the cup to Anselm. He thanked her and stretched out his legs on the stool that she placed before him. With a glance, he bade her to continue.

The old woman, she explained, lived alone on the island. She kept geese, but being indolent, never led them out to graze. One morning she took Laurence to the pen and, pointing at her gaggle, proposed an arrangement.

"A web-footed creature has swallowed my gold ring," she said. "Try to recognize the one that did, and kill it. If you guess right, and in its stomach you find the ring, I will give it to you. If not, you must remain here for a season as my servant."

The girl agreed, and began to observe the geese. There were more than one hundred, each one trumpeting at the top of its lungs. They all seemed in robust health but one, which kept its distance from the others and did not graze. Her choice fell upon this goose. She grabbed it by the throat, wrung its neck and brought it into the kitchen where she bled and eviscerated it. Alas, no ring was to be found, either in its stomach or in its intestines. She resigned herself to her fate, and under the direction of the widow, set to work. She transformed the sacrificed goose into comfit and potted meat. She weeded the vegetable patch, washed the sheets, kneaded the bread, wove fascines, gutted and dried herrings. All the while, the widow lay about in the sunshine. At summer's end, she made the same proposal.

This time, Laurence killed a bird whose neck appeared crooked. But there was no trace of a ring to be found. So Laurence harvested eelgrass to stuff the mattresses, plucked the goslings for their down and made up comforters. Through the autumn, she studied the geese on their way to pasture with such close attention that she was able to give each one a name. One by one she shook them until she could hear the tinkle of gold. When time came to renew their pact, she was certain that she had identified the right one. But once again luck abandoned her. She spent the winter splitting wood, shoveling snow, breaking the ice in the well and knitting stockings. And the widow lay there, contemplating herself in a mirror, content at having struck such an excellent agreement. When spring returned, she announced that she would take a bath. The girl heated the bathwater and poured it into a tub.

"While I am bathing," said the old woman, "go out into the fields. The serviceberries are in bloom. Bring me a few branches."

The girl obeyed. By the time she returned to the hut, the old woman had gone back to her bed. When she stepped from her bath, she left a trail of footprints on the floor, from tub to bed. And those footprints, flat and broad, were shaped like fans. Laurence dropped the branches she had collected and leaned over the old woman.

"Now I know which web-footed creature swallowed the gold ring," she said.

Throwing back the blanket, she uncovered the old woman's feet. She had not been mistaken: they had the flared shape of a goose, and the toes were connected by a membrane. The old woman writhed in anger.

"I swallowed my ring when the English came ashore, so they wouldn't steal it from me. If you want it, you'll have to slit my belly open."

Laurence was happy enough to regain her freedom. But as she left the hut, she threw open the door to the goose pen, and all the birds fled.

Anselm's father reacted to her story with disbelief.

"She has webbed feet herself," he accused her. "Can't you see she waddles like a duck?"

Yet as he watched Laurence go about her business, Anselm found her walk quite effortless. He had not been the object of such kind attention since the days when his mother still lived. With no hesitation, he asked the girl to spend the night beneath their roof.

"Take my room," he told her, "and I will sleep next door. My father stays here, close to the fire. Upstairs, you will not be disturbed."

The following day, when the stone carver returned from his workshop, he found the table already laid, and atop it a bowl of soup, a basket of hot bread and a pot of fresh butter. Laurence's eyes were sparkling, and her smile was inviting. Her hair fell in ringlets around her shoulders. She had hung out her clothing to dry before the fire and put on an ecru-colored woolen gown that Anselm immediately recognized, since he had seen his mother wear it on festive occasions, just as he recognized the pale green ribbon around her waist, and the lace scarf around her neck. His father complained bitterly at the shameless way she had rummaged through the belongings of his deceased spouse. But Anselm had given Laurence permission to take whatever struck her fancy.

He also asked her if she would care to stay with them a while. He did say it would be only fair were she to contribute something in exchange for her room and board. If she would look after the old man and the house, he would excuse her from the harsher tasks. She agreed with good grace. Anselm's father quickly rejected the idea. But after tasting Laurence's soup—a bouillon of wild roots flavored with sea lovage—he stopped voicing any objections.

The stone carver stopped and turned to Titus.

"The presence of a woman in the kitchen," he assured him, "is truly a tonic for two men who have lived alone for too long."

The farmhand threw him a knowing glance. The virtues of Madam McEvoy's soups were not unknown to him. In a moment of pity, Lily once secretly brought him a bowl, after he'd been sentenced to bread and water by the Rear-Admiral for having come too close to the manor. Though he found it a bit too salty, the wild root soup, which had grown cold on its way from the kitchen to the stable, had comforted, even consoled him.

As for the tonic effects of Madam McEvoy's personality, Titus allowed himself a doubt, though, by his own admission, he had only seen her up close a single time. Ever since his young age, he was strictly forbidden to show himself in her presence. Sundays, when she would go to Mass, the Rear-Admiral would lock the farmhand in the barn, allowing him out only after night had fallen. Titus noticed that, on those days, the sky would cloud over, flowers would droop and birds would cease their chirping. Were Madam McEvoy to venture too close to the barn, the cows' milk would curdle.

He caught the occasional glimpse of her when she received guests at the manor, when the candelabra in the parlor blazed. He would observe the festivities from a distance, perched in the branches of a tree. On one occasion, he had been daring enough to take up position in the flowerbed beneath the bay window of the parlor. There, hidden in the rose bushes, he even heard the conversations, for it was a warm evening and the windows were thrown open wide. The festivities were in full swing. Father Compain had come all the way from Beaumont for the event, and would spend the night at the manor. The neighbors had also been invited: Captain Alexander Fraser, whom the Rear-Admiral had met during the siege of Quebec, and who had just purchased the Seigneurie de Beauchamp; the Cullens of Saint Malachy with their four daughters; Patrick Boyce from Bois-Cajetan; the Odells of Ennis River ... Surely Titus had forgotten some of them.

The Rear-Admiral, in parade dress, was standing close to the hearth as was his custom, one boot propped atop the grate. He was drawing the attention of the ladies to his wife's jewelry. Contrary to what appearances might suggest, he explained, this was not a diamond aigrette at all, but a simple leafless service-berry twig which, after being soaked in a saline solution, had formed scintillating crystals as it dried.

Madam McEvoy was seated back to the window, and Titus could not see her face. She was wearing a sky blue gown, and white satin slippers that shone like two pearls against the oyster gray carpet. For all the heat, she held tight about her shoulders an otter-belly cloak. She took little part in the conversation, barely responding to questions that were put to her, preferring for the most part simply to nod her head. Her voice—here, Titus would have borne Master Anselm out—had something sandy about it, as did the sound of her harp when she accompanied her husband.

The Rear-Admiral had sung long and often that evening, old Irish laments and sea shanties. At the end of the concert, he bowed to all those present, basking in the applause of his guests. Madam McEvoy did not appear to have heard a thing. Overwhelmed by the heat, yet refusing to remove her cloak, she had come to the window, and was fanning herself furiously.

It was the first time Titus had seen her so close at hand, and he was struck by the hardness of her otherwise gracious face. That hardness came not only from her frozen features, but from the perfect smoothness of her skin. No wrinkle or imperfection offered a hold to the eye that might wish to scale its escarpments. Repelled by this face that was as inhospitable as a cliff, Titus

retreated. Madam McEvoy sensed the movement. More insidi-
ous than still water that conceals hidden currents, she spied Titus
through the darkness and fixed her eyes upon him, first with
indifference, then with cruelty and disdain. Transfixed, the farmhand fell to the ground, then waiting no further, fled on all fours.

The following night he could not return to his listening post.
A bear trap had been set in the midst of the rosebushes.

Master Anselm paid scant attention to Titus's story, and showed
no more sympathy for him than was warranted by the circumstances.

"It makes perfect sense that catching sight of an ordinary
farmhand would have offended a woman vain enough to wear
a fur cloak in the heat of summer," he said. "Laurence was not
fated to remain a servant, I can assure you of that, any more than
she intended to spend the rest of her life in Beaumont."

No sooner had the girl settled into the house, he said, than
she began to put on airs and behave like a princess. She would
awaken when the sun was already high in the sky, and take her
breakfast in bed. It would take her hours to finish her toilette,
to arrange her hair and tie her ribbons. She would spend the
afternoon on the shoreline, weaving tresses of blue mussels, and
bracelets of sandwort. She always had a good reason for sparing
herself the household chores: the washwater irritated her hands,
the dust caused her to sneeze, the broom gave her blisters ...
Only the kitchen did not repulse her, perhaps because she
amused herself by preparing dishes of algae and other marine
plants that she would harvest along the shore line: rosettes of
cabbage kelp with eel pie, boiled meats garnished with garden

lovage, sprigs of salicorne in pumpkin purée ... Anselm's father, before eating, would make sure to rid his plate of this "riverswill," as he called it. Instead of the jellies she would make with a red algae called dulse, he preferred a simple ladleful of molasses into which he would dip his bread.

"I ate with a hearty appetite," said Anselm, "seeing as I was fully occupied in the workshop. Business had picked up after the spring thaw and the reopening of the Port of Quebec—all thanks to the increase in the number of shipwrecks."

The Beaumont littoral, he explained, was made of coves where the low tide deposited whatever the river had swallowed up. Whenever bodies were found, the parish, in its generosity, took upon itself their burial. The vicar would order gravestones from Anselm upon which he would, more often than not, simply carve the word *Unknown*. In the early days of May 1770, a ship carrying a cargo of wine and spirits for several private individuals ran aground on the sandbar. Five men, including the captain, had lost their lives. Some time later, the corpses of three unfortunate fishermen whose bark had sunk off Trois-Rivières were identified. Since then, hardly a week went by that did not bring Beaumont its ration of drowned bodies. The vicar wrote to the governor requesting his assistance in defraying the costs of burial, which were threatening to become a veritable burden for the parish.

Laurence, in the course of her daily strolls along the shoreline, had discovered all the bodies. Anselm pointed out how precious her aid was, hoping to moderate his father's criticism of her.

"More precious than you think," the old man replied. "She's the one who's causing the shipwrecks."

River nymphs, according to him, had the reputation of sinking the barks that ventured too close to the sandbars by gnawing through their hulls.

"But Laurence's teeth are tiny!" Anselm protested. But he knew better: the shorter the knife, the sharper it cuts.

Talking all the while, the stone carver led Titus to the far reaches of the great room, which led into the main gallery of the mine. The retaining wall above the opening was decorated with a pediment illustrating the Rear-Admiral's exploits: the capture of *La Galante* off Cabo de Gata, the passage up the Saint Lawrence, the discovery of the salt spring, and finally, the nuptial ceremony in the cathedral.

As he examined the figure of the young bride in bas-relief, Titus noticed more than a few resemblances to that of Our Lady of the River, the one who stood in the Beaumont chapel. He set about enumerating them: the head held high, the shoulders thrown back, the throat festooned with necklaces, the fur cloak that fell to her feet.

"So, you know my altarpiece?" said Master Anselm. "Is it not admirable?"

"It would not bring umbrage to a cathedral," answered the farmhand, irritated.

"For all that, Monsignor Briand, who had commissioned it for the archiepiscopal see, did not want it."

In the bishop's eyes, in fact, the subject had been irreverently treated. "Our Lady is quite respectable as she is," he had written Anselm on returning the altarpiece to him, "without her being burdened with all kinds of attributes, and should be quite enough for the devotions of the faithful, especially if she is well carved."

"That is why I gave it to the parish of Beaumont," said Master Anselm. "Vicar Compain also refused to display it in the church. He relegated it to the processional chapel. But that is of no importance. Instead, let me tell you how the idea came to me."

Laurence had been living in Beaumont for more than a year when Anselm received the commission from Monsignor Briand, who wished to raise an altarpiece devoted to Our Lady of the River in the chapel of the bishop's residence. His sole instructions were that "the representation be characterized by grace and modesty."

Anselm had set aside a block of blue slate for just such an occasion. He discovered it one rainy afternoon when, as his father napped, Laurence had taken him for a stroll along the cliffs, as far as Pointe à l'Ardoise. From the promontory, their gaze encompassed the entire mouth of the Boyer River. Laurence, shivering beneath her sealskin cloak, pointed out the white bellies of a romp of otters disporting themselves in the water below.

"What lovely fur," she exclaimed. "How warm it would keep me!"

Sighing, she moved on ahead, head held high, to the farthest extremity of the point. Toes clinging to the very edge of the escarpment, she threw back her shoulders to maintain her balance and keep from toppling over the precipice. The posture thrust her bust forward. Standing there erect and nearly motionless, overlooking the river, she appeared for all the world like the figurehead of a ship. In Anselm's mind, that image remained associated with the blue slate he had brought back from the point, and he had no need to seek any further for the subject of the altarpiece he was about to begin.

The weeks during which he had worked on the commission proved to be fecund indeed. He was in such total mastery of his art that he did not bother to fashion a plaster model. He began working directly on the slate itself which, in his hands, became almost malleable. Instinctively grasping its structure, with its sheets and foliations, he devised a way to separate the layers of schist while leaving the desired motif in relief. In each stone, he told Titus, there lies as specific point which, when struck at the correct angle and with the necessary force, can reveal a sculptural element in its entirety. Four blows from the little hammer were all it took to sculpt a wave, a foot, a rock. In less time than it would have taken to rough out a pediment, he completed the bas-relief, from sketch to completed work.

Laurence, in the meantime, grew more recalcitrant. Every evening, after the old man retired, she joined Anselm in the workshop with her seal cloak and her necklaces. Though she readily assumed the pose, she refused to remove her clogs. With the excuse that she presented too much volume for a bas-relief, the stone carver stepped up to her and, with all his strength, crushed her against the wall. He took great care, however, not to disturb her hair, for had he done so, she would have fled. He believed that women, like slate, have their own foliations, their own point of resolve, which if touched with the proper pressure, would cause them to yield. Search though he might for Laurence's, he could not find it.

Master Anselm moved into the gallery, for the visit was in no way at an end. Titus followed close behind, almost treading on his heels. He had begun to feel revulsion at the display of Master Anselm's accomplishments, and at the thought of what his own masterwork might have been had fate not decided otherwise. He could not help thinking how much finer his craft would have been, and the resentment he felt towards the stone carver quickly grew. Above all, he felt disdain for Master Anselm's inability to detach his figures entirely from the support upon which they rested for, despite never having compared the merits of bas-relief and high contrast, he intuited that the greatness of a sculptor was to be judged by his determination to present his subject in all its aspects. The indifference that the stone carver affected towards everything that lay hidden behind the façade no longer appeared to him just as an artistic limitation, but a particular trait of character as well, a trait he was tempted to associate with a certain form of cowardice.

If the grove and pediment of salt had awakened Titus's long-sleeping indignation, the spectacle at the other end of the gallery thoroughly revolted him. It was there, in the secondary room of the mine, that he had long ago pilfered a block of salt. He could remember still its mass and its weight, particularly as he had lifted it, then hidden it in his shirt in order to spirit it out. His recollection of the chamber itself was vague. This much was clear: it had undergone many changes since then.

Master Anselm had transformed it into a pantheon of salt, a circular structure of approximately thirty feet in diameter, topped by a coffered dome of equal height. Into the thick walls deep niches had been carved, alternating between the rounded and the rectangular, separated by eight fluted pilasters formed by the protruding walls of the niches. The base of the dome was perforated with a series of windows which, though blind, were nonetheless decorated with cameos of salt, depicting various picturesque scenes of the Armagh estate beneath a mantle of snow: the manor house, the salt cellar, the farm, the orchard, the entrance to the mine, the salt works on the banks of the Loutre River ...

The niches themselves were carved out to form chapels. In the first one, to the right of the entrance, an altar was carved into the salt so as to create the impression that it was in reality an assemblage of human bones. The other chapels, as far as Titus could see in the torchlight, were furnished in an equally macabre fashion.

"What kind of place is this?" he asked, confused.

"Have you not yet understood?" said Master Anselm. "It is a funerary monument to Rear-Admiral McEvoy and his spouse. I built it according to the wishes and specifications of Her Excellency."

So that was their great secret, the farmhand fumed in silence. So that was the mysterious tie that bound them. This monument of overweening ambition, pomposity and pretentiousness was all the more ridiculous, in that no one would ever lay eyes on it. Lily had devoted the best years of her life to this vain enterprise, and Master Anselm, the last of his strength. Titus would have burst out laughing had he not felt so irritated. What wouldn't he have given to be the one to whom Lily entrusted the building of this mausoleum ... He, better than Master Anselm, knew what the Rear-Admiral's memory truly warranted. A reconstruction of all the torments of Hell!

"Well, what do you say?" queried the stone carver proudly.

"Salt does not last as long as stone," replied the farmhand with thinly disguised hostility. "Before long, nothing will remain of what you have built here."

Master Anselm lowered his eyes, an expression of exhaustion on his face. He knew the truth of what Titus had said far better than anyone else. Unlike limestone, sandstone or any of the other stones he had already worked in, the salt of the mine had proven itself soft, almost too easy to sculpt. This ease had been, in its own way, the reason why he had followed Lily into her every excess.

When Her Excellency had invited him to come work at the estate, her letter made mention of two simple stone crosses, engraved with short inscriptions. It was to be "an extremely modest monument," in her words. Master Anselm, believing that he would not be away from Beaumont for long, put aside his work at the parish house and, of all his stratigraphic instruments, brought only a compass and a protractor.

The journey to Armagh seemed to him long. Titus decided it would be better to ignore his questions, and not engage in conversation. Since they departed Beaumont, he had not removed his hands from his pockets except to wind the reins around his forearms, and guided the carriage with twists of his shoulders, at the risk of letting the horses stray from the road. Master Anselm felt certain that he had vexed the boy a few hours earlier, in the workshop. But not being a man to offer apologies, he blamed Titus instead for his excessive sensitivity. When one is afflicted with an infirmity, he reasoned, one must learn to suffer the stares of others without taking offense.

Upon arriving at the boundaries of the estate, the horses, catching the scent of the stable, began to strain at the bit, and Titus was forced to use his hands to rein them in. Master Anselm realized, first with curiosity, then with fascination, that those hands were not so much deformed as flattened, in the sense that they presented almost no protuberances. They looked, in fact, like hands depicted in ancient bas-reliefs. The broad palms, that looked as though they had been planed down, formed, along with the fingers with their crushed joints and concave nails, two ailerons that hung from the ends of his arms, and flapped in the slightest breeze. The infirmity could certainly not have been congenital, for the backs of his hands were copiously scarred. Even with an effort of imagination, the stone carver could not imagine what might have caused the wounds.

When they finally reached the main gate of the estate, Master Anselm asked to get out of the carriage. Though Titus advised him that the manor house was some distance away, he preferred to arrive on foot.

"In that case," said the farmhand, "bear to the left. It's a shortcut."

The ill-kept pathway twisted and turned through the forest. Accustomed to cleared land, Anselm recognized neither the scent of the air, nor the color of the sky, nor the cries of the birds. He felt as though he were in some foreign land. Insects unfamiliar to him buzzed about his head. He halted in the middle of a meadow, from which eight paths radiated. The trees around him were dismayingly similar. By dint of turning around in circles, he no longer could tell where he had come from. At the thought that he was lost in this inhospitable place, his heart turned cold. The sun was declining behind the hilltops. Night would soon fall. He had almost made up his mind to call for help when, behind him, a branch cracked. Suddenly, two yellow dogs leapt out from the thicket. They would have flown at him had not an imperative voice, at a single command, called them off.

It was Her Excellency who, not having seen Master Anselm arrive, set out to look for him.

She approached him and looked him straight in the eye, hoping to determine with whom she would be dealing.

"How did you find your way to this place?" she queried him, in the same brusque tone she used on the dogs.

"Your farmhand told me it was a shortcut."

"He most certainly misled you. You are on the path to the mine, which has been designed to confuse intruders."

There, in the mist of dying day, he believed that he beheld Laurence before him. Not that the young lady resembled her mother that strongly, but good blood will out. She had the same haughty cock of the head, the same abrasive voice, the same way of gripping her shawl tight about her shoulders.

"I have placed at your disposition a hut not far from here, where you can work undisturbed," she told him. "If you would like to follow me, I will lead you there."

The hut was clean; its walls had recently been whitewashed. It contained a table, a chair and a bed, peat in the hearth, an ample supply of candles, as well as bread, cheese and smoked fish in the larder. Nothing in Her Excellency's frigid hospitality revealed the slightest intention to lodge the stone carver any longer than necessary.

She waited until the following day to lead him to the mine. She wished to show him, she said, exactly where the funerary monuments were to be erected. Strolling through the pillars of salt, she deplored their appearance of neglect, and their protrusive angles that pointed to the scant attention given them by the miners who had roughed them out. Would it not be possible, she asked, to polish them a little?

Several days later, she announced her intention to transform the great room into a funeral garden by giving the columns the rough-textured appearance of tree trunks. Anselm did not resist the call to begin work, just as, later, he would turn his attention to the vault.

On the pretext of bringing him food, Her Excellency came to visit him each week in the mine. The reason was always the same: to submit to him a new project. Day after day, the tasks to be accomplished multiplied as if by themselves, each one generating an infinite number of new ideas that immediately took root in Lily's mind. Her thirst for ornamental details seemed unquenchable. "A few more garlands, Master Anselm. And why not some vine branches?" In the unchanging atmosphere of the mine, where the temperature never fluctuated, he worked unstintingly, never noticing the passing of the seasons.

After four years had gone by, with the great room decorated in its entirety and no more salt remaining to be carved, Her Excellency had him undertake the pediment of the gallery. She considered it unthinkable to stop when all was going so well. The secondary room, after all, awaited nothing more than Master Anselm's chisel …

For ten years, he confided to Titus, he had been the hand that carried out the desires of Her Excellency. He had been nothing more and nothing less than a slave, at the beck and call of her every requirement. Most of the time, she seemed to be fervently pursuing an ideal of perfection whose loftiness she alone could judge. Some days, however, the stone carver could have sworn that she was looking for things for him to do, to keep him in the mine.

"Master Anselm," Titus allowed himself to utter, "you were always free to leave. Why did you bow to her every whim?"

Anselm looked for a pillar to lean against.

"For the simple reason," he said, mopping his forehead, "that one cannot refuse a second chance."

Not long after the consecration of the processional chapel, he said, during which vicar Compain had blessed the altarpiece devoted to Our Lady of the River, a visitor of some importance called upon Anselm's workshop. Magnus McEvoy, Rear-Admiral of the Fleet of His Majesty King George III and owner of the Armagh salt mine, was so tall that his head touched the door-frame. Though his graying beard betrayed his forty-five years, he had the ramrod posture of a young ensign. He wore a broad-cut coat, waxed boots and a cocked hat with a gold medallion. He greeted Master Anselm, and his bass voice, accustomed to issuing orders from the bridge of a ship, echoed through the house.

He was naught but a seafaring man, he declared. His knowledge of sculpture was limited to little more than the meerschaum pipes that sailors carve. He himself had never possessed such a talent. But that did not mean he could not appreciate things of beauty. This morning, out of curiosity, he had entered the new chapel, and been troubled by the altarpiece he saw there. He had stood in front of it for some time, contemplating the image that reminded him of the figurehead of his former ship.

"Though I am Irish," he said, "I am not Catholic. But I would happily convert if I could prostrate myself before such a Holy Virgin as that one."

He begged Father Compain to sell him the piece, but the wicked vicar refused. The Rear-Admiral had to promise him a cargo of salt before he would agree to reveal the name of the sculptor.

"I have come here," he informed Anselm, "with the intention of commissioning a faithful replica."

He had built a residence of stone on the lands of the Armagh estate, he explained. It was far more sumptuous than the miserable seigneurial manor of Beaumont, and would have rivaled the governor's mansion if the latter, out of jealousy, had not forbidden him from adding turrets. The centerpiece of the parlor was an immense stone fireplace which cried out for decoration.

"Come with me to Armagh," he enjoined Anselm. "I shall place all the stones of the manor at your disposal, should you desire. I will be your new protector. I am rich. I will pay whatever you ask."

No sooner had he spoken those words than Laurence appeared on the threshold of the workshop. She had thrown back the folds of her sealskin cape, leaving the curves of her bust exposed. Her throat was bedecked with necklaces, and she held her chin high, the better to display them. That very pose, which pushed her upper body forward, had awakened in Master Anselm's mind the image of Our Lady of the River. The Rear-Admiral must have had the same impression, for he moved towards her and, bending a knee, paid her his respects.

"Your Excellency is too kind," she responded in a timid voice that Anselm had never heard before. "I am but a humble cook here."

Hearing those words, Magnus McEvoy blanched.

"In that event, allow me to offer you some salt from my estate." He handed her a small pouch tied with leather thongs. "I would be honored were you to use it as best you see fit."

Laurence thanked him before gracefully withdrawing.

The Rear-Admiral turned to Anselm as soon as her back was turned.

"Her resemblance to the Virgin in the chapel is stupefying," he whispered. "You are even more skillful than I imagined."

Anselm saw him to his carriage, and promised to give more thought to his proposal. In truth, he had no intention whatsoever of moving to Armagh. He could not leave his father, who was going from bad to worse.

After the Rear-Admiral left, the stone carver went to the table and sat down, for it was the supper hour. His father, who did not like to see Laurence dressed in finery, was grumbling incompre hensibly by the fire; a word that sounded very much like "wench" kept recurring.

Was it the effect of the Armagh salt that Laurence had used to season the soup that evening? Whatever the case, Anselm seemed to rediscover the taste of his years of apprenticeship. With every spoonful, he sank deeper into his past. Strangely, and more frighteningly, desires and hopes he thought long forgotten and laid to rest awoke within him. Thoughts that had not entered his mind since his return to Beaumont—thoughts of a free life that would let him practice his art as he pleased—now assaulted his imagination.

"Think about it," he told Titus. "I finally met a man who recognized my talent, and who asked for nothing more than to encourage its development."

After his rebuff at the hands of his compatriots, and above all of Monsignor Briand, the Rear-Admiral's offer had been more than he could have hoped for, and certainly warranted the most attentive consideration. Why, indeed, could he not accept it? Nothing held him in Beaumont. There was his father, of course, but Laurence would look after him. As for her … He would send her money regularly, she would lack for nothing. He would return after a year, having made his fortune. They would move to Quebec City. He would open a workshop, take on apprentices. Perhaps he would even rise to the rank of senior surveyor ...

These were the thoughts that went through his mind, as his decision imposed itself with all the force of truth.

When he went to wish his father goodnight, the old man began to chortle, pointing to Laurence who had been standing, face to the window, all evening long.

"These river nymphs are like the tides," he muttered. "They come in, then they go out. Take my word for it, this one will soon be taking her leave."

At the time, Anselm had paid no heed to his ravings. Why would Laurence leave? Had he not always treated her well? Yet doubt had taken a foothold in his mind.

Despite the day's fatigue, he did not fall asleep easily. His father's words echoed in his mind like a market vendor's refrain. He had to admit that the plans he had drawn up with such ease had a weak point, and it was a substantial one. They rested upon the presumption that Laurence would remain in Beaumont for some time to come. If she packed up and left tomorrow, Anselm would have no choice but to forsake his aspirations. Yet the idea of following in his father's footsteps had become intolerable. There was only one way to ward off such an eventuality, and that was to keep Laurence close by. But he did not know how to proceed.

Illumination came to him in the middle of the night. Were he to marry her, she would have to take up residence with them! In fact, it was not even necessary to marry her. To promise was enough. An engagement would keep her in Beaumont at least a year ... When he returned from Armagh, there would always be time to break it off. His plan seemed so flawless that he could not wait to put it into action. He got up and sought out the girl in her room.

She had fallen asleep atop the blankets, fully clothed, enveloped in her cloak with only her two bare feet protruding. Anselm found himself trying to discover, in the darkness, whether or not they were webbed. Why not take advantage of the situation to examine them more closely, and put his doubts to rest? He slid his hand carefully along her feet until he reached the end.

"Then what?" asked Titus impatiently.

"My father was not mistaken," admitted Master Anselm. "Stretched between her toes, there was a kind of thick, granular membrane."

His pounding heart awakened Laurence. She sat bolt upright, uttering a cry of indignation. To silence her, he threw himself upon her.

"Don't worry," he reassured Titus. "I did her no harm."

But he did press her beneath him with such force that he all but turned her into a bas-relief. When he left, some time later, she seemed well disposed toward him. He withdrew to his workshop, confident that he had convinced her to stay.

"Come next morning," said Master Anselm, "she had packed her bags and vanished."

He was sure that she could not have gone far. He harnessed his horse and set off at a gallop for the mill at Vincennes, then turned north. He searched as far as Pointe de l'Ardoise. No one had seen her. He decided that she must have regretted her decision and returned home, so he headed back. But she was not there. His father mocked him.

"You're wasting your time. She's gone back to the river, and you'll never see her again."

He did not believe a word of it. But come evening, he went down to the shoreline and called out Laurence's name.

91

"Begging your pardon, Master Anselm," Titus piped up. "Did it ever occur to you that the Rear-Admiral might have abducted her?"

"It would have been easy for him to sneak into the house by night," admitted the stone carver. "However, Laurence would have resisted, and I would certainly have heard the noise."

"And what if she left with him of her own free will?"

"How could such a thing have been arranged? The two of them exchanged only a few words, and then only in my presence … Two beings who barely know each other cannot understand one another in silence, after all …"

"And yet," Titus pointed out, "she well and truly ended up at Armagh."

"She did indeed," conceded Master Anselm. "That, I was only to learn later."

Hardly a month had elapsed since Laurence's departure, he went on, when his father suffered another attack of apoplexy. This time, there was no hope of recovery. Anselm watched over him day and night and, terrible though it is to say, he did so hoping not to detect some sign of improvement, but to recognize the signs of decline. "Would it not be better for it all to end?" he found himself thinking. Though he tried to put it aside, the question of what he would do after his father's death constantly ran through his mind.

He was awakened one night by the sick man's whimpering, which seemed more feeble than usual. Perhaps the time had come to summon the priest, he thought. "I wish he was dead," he realized, in shame. As if to rid himself of those thoughts, he rolled over in bed and fell back asleep. The next morning, as soon as he opened his eyes, he knew he was alone in the house.

His father was buried in the Beaumont cemetery. Anselm dug the grave himself. The thought of erecting a funerary monument crossed his mind. But considering that the old man had not granted his own wife the privilege, he changed his mind. He could think of only one thing: close the workshop and leave for Armagh. The next day he wrapped his tools in a bundle, harnessed his horse and set out.

"If you look closely at these paving stones," Master Anselm told Titus, "you will see that I have reproduced the road that leads to the estate of Armagh."

The floor of the pantheon, he informed the farmhand, was entirely covered with tiny tiles of salt that, in their diverse forms and dimensions, composed a labyrinth. It was not a labyrinth to lose oneself, but rather one built on the model of those found in cathedrals, which invite the pilgrim to be guided, to trust the path laid down—and mistrust himself. Perfectly set, the path wound its way through eight concentric rings, encompassing the entirety of the space within the circle, making its way past an image of the village of Beaumont, crossing brooks and rivers and leading, at the end of its meanderings, to one of the niches in the pantheon.

"This crossroads," he said, indicating a point within the labyrinth, "represents the Station of the Cross at La Hêtrière. It was there that I discovered Laurence's tracks."

He had met a farmer cutting his hay, and paused to ask him where the road to Armagh might be. The old man gave him vague directions, and enquired what he intended to do there. "You don't look like a miner," he ventured warily. Anselm told him he was a stone carver, and was going to work at the manor. Apparently, he was the second traveler within two months to ask directions of the farmer. A young girl had come this way before him, going to the estate as well. She had come from Beaumont, and seemed to have difficulty walking. Taking pity on her, the farmer invited her into his cart and drove her as far as the Sault.

Laurence, Anselm concluded, had indeed followed the Rear-Admiral, undoubtedly hoping to be offered a position of cook in his household.

He was about to continue on his way when the farmer called out to him. Was it true, he asked, that McEvoy was being married today? The rumor had spread throughout the township that he had converted for the occasion, and that Monsignor Briand himself would officiate at the ceremony in the Quebec cathedral. It was being said as well that there would be a wedding party at the manor, which was to be attended by Governor Carleton and all the notables from the environs. No one knew the fiancée, for she was not from the area. But everyone claimed that she was a young lady of distinction, born of one of our long established families. If the Irish start stealing our women, the old man added, what will become of us?

In his haste to reach Armagh before the wedding feast, Anselm bid the farmer goodbye and hastened his pace.

He had stopped to water his horse at the Sault. Soon, he heard the clatter of wheels drawing near. He did not have to wait long: a good thirty carriages passed before him. This was the nuptial cortege, making its way back from Quebec City.

He followed from a distance, and reached the main gate of the manor just as twenty naval artillery officers were taking up positions on each side of the road, forming a guard of honor with swords drawn.

At the entrance to the estate, it was as if winter had suddenly arrived. Everything was white: the ground, the trees, even the pillars of the main gate. The whiteness gleamed like snow in the sunlight, and filled the air with constellations of tiny, piercing lights whose darting rays gave the eye no respite.

Anselm was admiring the landscape when he heard a grumbling voice behind him.

"McEvoy has dusted everything with salt, and why? To impress a woman!"

It was Monsignor Briand. He recognized the stone carver and had come over to greet him in a state of high dudgeon.

"So, the Rear-Admiral has converted," Anselm commented.

"The pagan's conversion is not his cure, but at most, his convalescence," the bishop said, bending over to scoop up some salt, with which he filled his pockets. "Such a man may fall back at any moment. The wife he has chosen is far from being a model of grace and modesty."

He pointed to the bride, who was stepping down from the coach. Anselm almost fell from his horse. There, on the Rear-Admiral's arm, was Laurence! There was no mistaking her. Beflowered and bejeweled, she was moving forward up the entryway with her slightly limping step.

The stone carver felt such anger rise within him that he made no effort to conceal it. So, while he was stuck back in Beaumont because of Laurence's desertion, the traitorous woman used the advance she'd gained to usurp his place at the manor. To all appearances, Armagh was the theater of a malicious feminine intrigue in which the Rear-Admiral, either out of naivety or disillusionment, had been the plaything. Perhaps the river nymph made him forget that he once planned to decorate his fireplace with bas-reliefs, by convincing him that he now possessed the living model of Our Lady of the River. Whatever the case, Anselm was not to be so easily pushed aside. He would remind Magnus McEvoy of their undertaking straightaway.

He dismounted, but could proceed no farther. Monsignor Briand had grabbed him by the shirttails.

"Where are you going in such a state?" he asked him.

Anselm answered that he had to speak to the Rear-Admiral without delay. The bishop stopped sniffing the salt dusting the air long enough to answer him.

"I heard him order the soldiers to keep you out. This gate is closed to you, Anselm. Your services are no longer needed here, and you are not welcome. Come back and work for me. You will not regret it."

The stone carver freed himself from Briand's grasp and moved on the cortege. But faced with the evil look of the soldiers, he quickly showed his heels.

Back at the bishop's side, he inquired, "If I agree to work for you, will you let me decorate the tympanum of the cathedral?"

"We shall see. In the meantime, take these eight pieces of gold."

"It is too much, Monsignor."

"It is not for you, of course. You will use it to purchase a fine Acadian amethyst, from which you will sculpt me a vial."

And so Anselm returned to Beaumont, but he would not admit defeat.

"One way or another," he swore, "I shall return to Armagh."

After their wedding day, Master Anselm never saw either Laurence or the Rear-Admiral alive. Still, he told Titus, he had ample opportunity over the last ten years to contemplate their bodies.

"Are they really buried in the mine, as Father Compain claims?" asked the farmhand.

"A funerary monument would not be complete without the deceased," Anselm responded.

A bony sound suddenly echoed in the lofty vault of the pantheon. That was Titus cracking his knuckles, with his hands still deep in his pockets.

"I would like to pray at the Rear-Admiral's grave," he said.

"It is in the crypt."

"Is there any way to get there?"

"Nothing could be simpler," said Master Anselm. "Follow the labyrinth."

Titus set out along the path drawn on the paving stones, which led him to one of the niches. Behind the altar an opening had been made. It was so low he had to stoop to pass through it. Master Anselm followed him in silence. Making their way down several steps, they entered an undecorated hall lit by a candelabrum carved in salt, each of the pendants of which was shaped like a teardrop. The candlelight, refracted through these transparent drops, flowed in long swaths over two caskets that lay at the center of the crypt. Both, it goes without saying, were carved out of salt, and their lids were decorated with reliefs representing the Rear-Admiral and his wife taking their eternal rest. Titus could not help wondering how Master Anselm had been able to make them so incredibly life-like, both in face and profile.

"I had the models close at hand," replied the stone carver. "Here, help me swing this cover open."

The inside of the casket was filled with coarse salt. Master Anselm brushed aside the uppermost layer with the back of his sleeve. Titus jumped back when he saw the Rear-Admiral's mummified face. The dead man's flesh, stretched tight over his bones, had the darkened, shriveled appearance of dried meat.

"Do you want me to open Madam McEvoy's casket as well?" asked Master Anselm.

"That won't be necessary," answered Titus.

"Both of them were bled, rubbed with saltpeter and packed in salt in an identical manner. They have become desiccated, but have been spared decomposition, and their features have lost nothing of their essence."

"Did you salt them yourself?"

"Oh no!" objected the stone carver. "They were in this state when I arrived. I believe the Rear-Admiral salted his wife's body, and that Lily and her two servants, Ursula and Perpetuity, tended to his."

Salt, which has the property of absorbing moisture, had affected his own health in like manner, he confessed to Titus. After ten years in the mine, his skin was as weathered as that of the Rear-Admiral's. His eyes had turned opaque, as if stricken with cataracts. The fine particles of salt made his breathing laborious. His muscles had shriveled to such a point that he could no longer lift his arms; in fact, he had been unable to attach the final pendant to the chandelier that hung in the crypt.

But this was nothing compared to the strange transformation the salt had worked upon his soul. When the stone carver considered his life, it was with a bitterness that left a briny taste in his throat. He thought often of Lily and her unyielding desire to build this monument to her parents' memory.

"Such devotion is admirable in a child," he said. "I, who have no descendants, cannot but envy these two salted bodies. Even though I have carved gravestones for others all my life, when I die there will be no one to erect even so much as a humble marker over me."

The question had begun to torment him, now that his sojourn at Armagh was for all intents and purposes over. Soon he would return to Beaumont, where he would live out his days in solitude.

Titus went to his side as if to console him.

"If I promised to raise a monument upon your death," he said, "would you tell me the secrets of your trade?"

"What would you do with them, since your fingers are good for nothing?"

"I still have the strength of my arms."

With a push of his shoulder, he closed the casket lid. But his demonstration was far from over. Withdrawing from his pocket his right hand, to which a short-bladed knife was attached with a tight harness, he began to correct Master Anselm's portrait of the Rear-Admiral. In less time than it took to castrate a chick, and with a skill that astonished the stone carver, he hollowed the eye sockets where the lids came together, scraped away the nose and carved out the cheeks. In place of the lips, he fashioned two rows of teeth to form what was now a death's head.

"Now," he said, "your work is truly complete. Come, Master Anselm, it's late, and you're expected at the manor."

III

TITUS

Sitting in front of the faded mirror of her room, Lily was powdering herself as if she had all the time in the world. She dipped her puff into a box of fine salt, retouching first her temples, then her neck, in an attempt to hide the blue veins and the faint pink that still tinged her cheeks. Her eyebrows and eyelashes, heavy with agglutinated salt, gave her the terrified look of an ermine surprised by a winter storm. The saline powder filtered down onto her shoulders, sifted between the gathers of her corset, disappeared among the yellowed folds of her white gown, the selfsame gown her mother had worn on her wedding day and which, on Lily, seemed to billow like a rudderless vessel.

Drawing close to the mirror, she looked at herself. Immediately, she frowned and threw down her powder puff angrily. Her efforts had simply drawn attention to the darkness of her gaze, which might in turn betray her intentions. Well, in that case, she would just have to keep her eyes lowered, since it was too late to remove her makeup. The voices of Ursula and Perpetuity rose up from downstairs, along with the clinking of plates and utensils. What were they talking about? Surely about her, or Master Anselm. Getting soundlessly to her feet, she tiptoed to one of the hatchways that her father had installed in the floorboards. She raised the trapdoor silently, and leaned over the opening to see what was going on in the dining room below.

Perpetuity was setting the table, while Ursula sharpened the carving knife. The fabric covers had been removed from the chairs, and the candles of the candelabrum had already been lit.

"Look, the tablecloth is still yellow," said Ursula.

"And I rinsed it three times."

"You should have whitened it with salt."

"With salt? But it's the salt that ruined it. And linen of such fine quality it is, one of the loveliest pieces from Madam Laurence's trousseau."

"Pardon me," Ursula corrected her. "Madam had no trousseau when she arrived. The Rear-Admiral had brought over the Irish linens, the porcelain, the crystal and the silver well before he met her ·.... Only her wedding gown was made in Quebec City. Did you remember to take it out of the trunk for airing?"

"Yes, but it is even yellower than the tablecloth."

"Just as well. Her Excellency is too old to wear white."

"Don't talk so loud. She'll be coming down any minute now. I wager she's standing right behind the door, even as we speak."

"I have a sensitive ear. I would have heard her."

"Your sensitive ear must have been blocked this morning when she caught us by surprise in the kitchen."

"She didn't surprise us, since she didn't punish us."

"It's only because she had her mind on that man, Anselm. If he becomes master of the house, maybe we won't have to hide when we eat sugar."

"My dear Perpetuity, you're dreaming. Just because Her Excellency is inviting the Devil to supper doesn't mean she intends to marry him."

"Doubt all you want, Thomas. I'm telling you this evening will end with a wedding."

Lily closed the hatchway. She had heard enough. To make matters worse, she felt herself turning gloomy.

"This evening should be an occasion for rejoicing," she said to herself. "Why am I not more gay?"

She stepped to the window and pushed aside the curtains. The sun was setting with all deliberate speed behind the creaking weathercock of the stable, whose shadow had now reached the mud puddles that dotted the roadway. This was the hour that Titus usually led the cows back from pasture. Hat pulled low over his head, he would walk along, staring at the ground, never allowing his eyes to stray in the direction of the manor though it was obvious, judging by the circumspection with which he guided the beasts, with a touch of his switch to their rumps, that he knew Lily was watching him. Why did she go to such lengths, day after day, to spy on him? Surely because she took pleasure in tormenting herself. Each time he came into view from behind the copse of ash, she would picture, with the precision of a torturer, the fateful morning when, from this same observation post, she saw Titus emerge from the woods and come to a halt beneath her window, raising his two bloody fists towards her in a gesture of accusation. The memory, which always brought a moan from her lips, was all the more painful for being exacerbated with a generous sniff of salt from her amethyst vial. It had become a nervous tic which she repeated once more, now with increased anxiety as clouds gathered on the horizon. This evening, would the heavens attempt to dilute, with drops of fresh water, the brine that she had devoted so many years to distilling?

Her gaze scanned the grounds, the orchard and, at the edges of the copse, the clearing from which issued the road to the mine. Not a soul to be seen. What was Titus doing? He had been gone for nearly five hours. Perhaps she had been a little cruel when she sent him so near to the salt works, knowing the tragedy that had taken place there so long ago. And had she not been imprudent to expose her valet to Master Anselm, to whom he might reveal things that still needed to be suppressed? Perhaps. But whatever Titus might reveal, it would do no more than raise a few suspicions in the stone carver's mind. And they would be so inadmissible that they would be swiftly dismissed as so many ravings, until the moment when Lily, with deceptive sweetness, would rekindle them, and confirm them all with one single, irrefutable proof.

That irrefutable proof was the bust sculpted by Titus which she had carried down from the attic a few hours earlier. Even after ten years, it had lost none of its brilliance. Though enveloped by the penumbra of declining day, it cast its iridescence into the far corners of the room, with all the turbulence of a truth about to break free. Lily approached it, caressed the stems of the lilies and the curves of the face; she traced the slope of the neck down to the hollow of the collarbones. Lily had filled this natural recess with fine particles of salt. She took a soupçon on her fingernail, for this particular salt would melt at the warmth of human fingers, and deposited it reluctantly upon her lips. She grimaced. The salt was more acrid than gall.

"Just as it should be," Lily declared, then made her way downstairs to the kitchen.

When she beheld her mistress moving toward the hearth, pallid in her pale gown, Ursula could not help but think of the phantom that prowled the corridors of the foundling home by the full moon, and that terrorized the residents by snapping long skin streamers in front of the windows.

"She has come to salt the food," the cook muttered. "Her mother did it with so much more finesse ..."

The day Ursula hired on at the manor, she tasted the Rear-Admiral's wrath for having failed to salt the soup. The dinner had hardly been served when His Excellency burst into the kitchen. Grasping the young maidservant by the skin of her neck, he dunked her face in the pot.

"What is this dishwater?" he roared.

Ursula protested vehemently: she had spiced the bouillon with the ash of sweet-scented tussilage. At the Ursulines, where she had trained for domestic service, it was used as a replacement for salt, which was reserved for the mother superior's table and kept under lock and key.

"You are no longer at the convent," the Rear-Admiral replied. "Here, I want the salt to flow abundantly."

The next time she forgot to salt the food, he warned her, he would fetch his cat-o'-nine-tails, and give her a whipping she would not soon forget.

"Off with you, go sob in the soup," he added when she burst into tears. "Your tears might give it some taste."

After that, Madam McEvoy herself would come to check the seasoning, not only of the soup, but of all the dishes. Shortly before the meal, she would make her appearance in the kitchen. From the salt box, she would take handfuls of salt, and cast it here and there, as if she were a magician casting spells.

"You see," she told Ursula, "you can make generous use of it. Water can absorb up to one fifth its volume of salt."

For all her attempts to imitate her, the cook could never add enough.

From Madam McEvoy, she learned that salt had many other virtues than those of a mere condiment. It made vegetables more toothsome, coffee less bitter and potatoes less starchy. It kept fruits from blackening, milk from souring and cheese from molding. It reduced the time water took to boil, cream to whip and egg whites to hold peaks. It killed the worms that lurked in cabbage. By soaking and scrubbing, it made shelling nuts and plucking chickens easier.

Salt had numerous other domestic uses, which Madam McEvoy did not fail to teach Perpetuity. It could be used for removing spots from porcelain and fabric, and from tarnished brass, silver and copper, wiping the soot from chimneys, scouring cast iron pots and irons, sterilizing sponges, cleaning brooms and wicker furniture …

Always smiling and indulgent, Madam McEvoy was sweetness itself toward her maidservants, at least during the first years of her marriage. Ursula and Perpetuity suffered grievously during the long months when, while awaiting the arrival of the first McEvoy child, she sequestered herself in the manor turret so that no one would see her in her condition.

Only the ground floor of the turret was inhabitable, and its atmosphere was frigid and humid. Madam McEvoy, wrapped in her otter-belly cloak, did not emerge from it a single time, all through the depths of winter. Ursula and Perpetuity would deliver her meals and laundry to her through the window. But when they ventured a glance inside, they didn't even see her shadow. The Rear-Admiral slept before his wife's door and, every morning, begged her to allow him to enter. But he was unfailingly dismissed, which drove him in turn to a fury. The two maidservants, at the mercy of his tantrums, lived through that period in a state of nameless terror, which came to a climax on Saint Patrick's Day, when Magnus McEvoy decided to tattoo the insignia of the estate, an *A* made of two picks and a sheet anchor, on their forearms.

One after the other, he led them down into the mine. There, by the light of burning faggots, and to the rhythm of a warrior's chant, a Pawnee slave punctured the skin of their right arms with a pike bone that had been soaked in a black substance, a mixture of gunpowder, castor oil and bear gall. The only way to erase a tattoo, the Rear-Admiral informed them, was to scrub it with coarse salt. But should they ever attempt to erase theirs, he would not hesitate to brand them with a red-hot iron.

With a quaver in the depths of her bosom, Ursula reached toward her tattooed arm, not quite touching it. All the while, Lily sprinkled salt into the soup. Any more and the contents of the entire box would end up in the pot. Ursula knew what the mistress would do next. She would drop an egg into the broth and make sure it floated—which meant that the decoction had attained the salinity of brine.

"She's worse than her father," Ursula said to herself. "And she'll end up the same way he did."

She still recalled the Rear-Admiral's death agony, when his tongue turned black. Even as Lily gave him water to drink, he complained of a parched throat. It was incomprehensible.

Upon the death of his wife, he made it known that he would not outlive her by more than a month. Perpetuity attributed his rapid decline to inconsolable grief. Ursula, the less emotional of the two, doubted that his illness was natural. When refilling the carafe in his room, she had noticed the white crystals at the bottom of the recipient. She realized that he was attempting to poison himself in the way shipwrecked sailors perish, by drinking salt water. She immediately sent Titus to Beaumont to seek out Father Compain. She was at the Rear-Admiral's bedside when the vicar confronted him.

"You are casting yourself without resource into eternal damnation by seeking to put an end to your life," he said.

With a groan, the Rear-Admiral replied, "I have lost my figure head. Why should I continue to exist?"

"The Church will deprive you of the succor of its prayers, and the honors of Christian burial if you persist. Repent, while there is still time."

But it was too late. The next day, Magnus McEvoy expired in Lily's arms.

When Ursula saw the vicar to his carriage, they spied the deer to which the Rear-Admiral had been giving salt. There on the grounds, they had formed a wide circle, facing the door. The vicar remarked that they were mourning the end of an era.

In the dining room, Perpetuity had almost completed the task of placing the glassware in such a way as to camouflage, to the best of her ability, the yellowed folds of the tablecloth. Lily had given her no indication of what she and her guest would be drinking, so she brought from the buffet the carafes, the wine glasses, the cider goblets, the small spirit glasses, the Madeira tulips (Madeira was the favorite beverage of the Rear-Admiral, who found wine too insubstantial). She had rinsed them in salty water, then polished them with kid gloves to a high gloss.

Perpetuity could still recall the day when the chests of glassware arrived from Ireland. She had unwrapped them herself. Miraculously, nothing on the inside had broken. Over the years, she had cared for those glasses so jealously that they all remained intact—except, of course, for the one that had shattered in the Rear-Admiral's hands when Perpetuity informed him that his wife had just given birth to a child.

In the muffled silence of the dining room, the sound of Lily's voice, ringing out from just behind her, made her jump.

"Put away the glasses and the carafes," she ordered. "We shall be having no need of them. You will put out the salt shakers in their stead."

"Which salt shakers, Your Excellency?" the maidservant asked with flagrant insincerity.

"My father's," replied her mistress, pointing toward the walnut sideboard with a determined finger.

The piece had not been opened since the Rear-Admiral's death. While he was alive, no one else was entitled to touch the salt cellars that, over the years, Master Anselm had sent him.

"I do not have the key," protested Perpetuity.

"The sideboard has never been locked," answered Lily.

Grumbling, the maidservant opened both doors of the sideboard. What manner of house was this, she mused, in which the sugar was locked away, but not the silverware?

But the salt shakers were not made of silver, for that metal corrodes and pits on contact with salt. They had been sculpted in various local minerals, including galena and pyrite, both of which have bright reflective surfaces. They were shaped like nacelles, and each was decorated with a relief depicting a famous ship: the *Argo*, the *Santa Maria*, the *Grande Hermine*, the *Batavia*, the *Sovereign of the Sea* ... Perpetuity had no idea which one she should choose.

"Bring them all out," ordered Lily.

They were nineteen in number. When Perpetuity, with infinite care, had lined them up on the table, Lily then deposited, exactly in the middle, the salt-carved bust she had brought down from the attic. In the flame of the candelabrum, it seemed to be ablaze. Dazzled, the maidservant averted her eyes and took a step backward. She had seen that bust once before, in the days following the death of Madam McEvoy.

Perpetuity remembered all too well. She was busy cleaning the room of the deceased when Lily came rushing in, holding in her embrace the glittering bust that the maidservant could not help admiring, in whose features she could recognize those of the young girl who was now making straight for the closet, having nearly wrenched its doors from their hinges. The inside of the closet was empty.

"The cloak?" Lily had cried out. "Where is the cloak?"

The otter-belly cloak had been stored in a wicker chest along with the rest of Madam McEvoy's clothing. Perpetuity hurried off to retrieve it and returned it to Lily, who immediately laid it out on the bed and folded it over upon the bust, making a tightly wrapped packet. The maidservant watched as she left the room and climbed up to the attic. She came down later, empty handed, and locked herself in her room. If Perpetuity was not mistaken, that was the day when she discovered Titus, unconscious in the barn, his hands drenched with blood.

Suddenly a muffled blow rang out, which seemed to come from the far reaches of the grounds. Lily's head snapped toward the window, as she attempted to see beyond the reflection of the candelabrum on the dark windowpanes.

"Is it a thunderstorm, Perpetuity?"

"No, your Excellency, someone is knocking at the door."

"Indeed? It has been so long since anyone has come here ... I forgot that the door knocker made such noise."

"Should I go to open?"

"No, tonight that task is incumbent upon me. Back to the kitchen now! Hurry!"

The maidservant was not unhappy to leave the dining room. The sight of so much salt made her thirsty. All she could think of was quenching it with a glass of spruce beer.

Once Perpetuity turned her back, Lily drew forth the amethyst vial. Her hands were clammy, her mind churned with confusion. She felt so lightheaded she was afraid she would faint.

"Just a pinch," she told herself. "So I forget nothing."

So saying, she took three sniffs.

Lily tugged with all her strength, and the door swung open. In the deepening darkness of dusk that had settled over the grounds, her eyes first sought out Titus. But he must have returned to the stable, since Master Anselm stood alone on the threshold. Lily could barely recognize him. He had washed his face and hands. His hair, freshly rinsed, clung in strands to his forehead. He had even put on an old frock coat and a ruffled shirt.

"He's put on his Sunday best," she thought in horror. "Let it not be for my sake."

How easy it had been, in the caverns of the mine, to forget the man's lowly extraction. She might issue the orders, but he ruled the works with his raspy voice, his pitch black hair and his muscular hands. More than once, she found herself observing him, even looking at him with an attention that bordered on admiration. But transplanted into the elegant surroundings of the manor, he was no more than a coarse artisan, clumsy and graceless, whose presence in Lily's proximity was almost insulting. In her discomfort, she did not deign, nor could she yet permit him to enter. And so she stepped out onto the porch.

"Is the candelabrum finished?" she asked.

"I was about to hang the last pendant when your farmhand came for me. I will complete it tomorrow."

"You will do nothing of the kind. It is of no importance."

Master Anselm was startled. Of no importance? The great candelabrum of the McEvoy family vault, upon which he had lavished the minutest care?

"There is an end to all things," declared Lily. "After ten years, the time has come to close the mine."

"This is what you have summoned me here tonight to tell me?"

Rather than answer, she came down the steps and began walking along the pathway. Master Anselm followed at a cautious distance. He could ill explain her sudden lack of interest in the funerary monument, and wondered what might lie behind her decision to bring the work to such an abrupt end.

"You have never before visited the manor, is that not correct?" Lily asked after a minute or two.

"I have never seen it except from a distance. What happened to the turret? Why is it in ruins?"

"It is not in ruins. It was never finished. By the fault of your former protector, Monsignor Briand."

The manor, she related, was built in 1768, when all the workers from the vicinity were still employed in the construction of the Quebec cathedral. Magnus McEvoy had complained to the bishop of the difficulties he had finding stone carvers, and his worship agreed to detach him seven.

"Were you not among them, Master Anselm?"

"At the time," he said, "I had already returned to Beaumont, to be close to my father."

"What a pity. The manor would have greatly benefited from your talents."

It had not taken long for the Rear-Admiral to certify that the prelate had sent him neither his best, nor his most conscientious workers. They frequently vanished without warning. Nor did they follow the plans, claiming they were unable to understand them. Matters had reached such a pass that the second story windows, which they had set far too low, seemed to crush those of the ground floor. They continually dropped entire shovelfuls of earth into the mortar trough, which could only be considered an act of sabotage.

"At this distance it is hard to detect the damage," Master Anselm told Lily. "But, knowing Monsignor Briand, I will certainly take your word for it."

The workers, Lily continued, turned out to be spies hired by the bishop. They kept him informed of the comings and goings of the Rear-Admiral, of his activity at the mine and of his future plans for the estate. They informed him of McEvoy's intention to construct turrets at each extremity of the manor house. These turrets, modeled on the Admiralty in London, would be topped with their own yardarms and rigging.

Alarmed by the magnitude of the work, Monsignor Briand complained to Governor Carleton of the excessive ambitions of Magnus McEvoy. He drew attention to the jealousy that the manor, which threatened to outshine the governor's residence itself, would be certain to arouse in all the nearby townships. He had no need to say more. Lord Carleton immediately sent a message to the Rear-Admiral ordering him to stop the work without delay, regardless of their state of completion.

At Armagh, however, the first of the turrets had already been built, as well as the staircase that led to its first two floors. The ground floor room had been outfitted with a fireplace in the same grand style as those of the main house. All that remained was to install the roof. Suspecting that the workers were spying for the governor, the Rear-Admiral flew into a rage. Drubbing them with a stick, he dispatched them back to their master, Monsignor Briand, paying them not a cent of what he owed them.

"Don't worry, Master Anselm," Lily quickly added after she finished. "No such thing will happen to you. You will receive exactly the salary you have earned."

She invited him into the house with a smile that was meant to reassure him, but given how quickly it faded from her face, it hardly achieved its purpose. As they made their way through the entrance hall, they passed in front of a portrait of Magnus McEvoy in uniform, with the sea and a frigate in the background. Though the resemblance was poor, the portrait revealed to perfection the Rear-Admiral's severe and rigid demeanor, the same that now suffused Lily's face.

"Master Anselm," she asked him, without taking her eyes off the portrait, "did you weep upon your father's death?"

"A little, though for me it was a deliverance."

"I shed not a tear, for I had prepared for it for months."

"Did it take him that long to die?"

"No. You see, a banshee had warned me of his death."

One day as she was returning from the mine, she related, she had been drawn by music of crystalline clarity echoing from the Loutre River. A washerwoman was crouched on the bank. The fabric she was slapping on the rocks was so bloodstained that the water had turned dark red. Hearing Lily draw near, she turned toward her, exposing her white eyes, her recessive upper lip and her teeth, which a silver wire kept in place.

"Banshees keen only for Irish families," said Lily. "Some of them have such a piercing cry that it can burst the eardrums. Others produce the sound of two boards being clapped together. The McEvoy banshee was like an Aeolian harp. She produced the sound of chimes when her breath set her teeth to vibrating."

"How did you know she was presaging the death of a McEvoy?" inquired Master Anselm.

"I recognized the bloodstained laundry that she held in her hands. It was my father's dress uniform."

She ushered Master Anselm into the parlor, whose sole source of light was a lingering fire in the hearth. The first time she had been allowed into this room, Lily said, she was seven years old. Her father had been entertaining a visitor, the fur trader Alexander Henry, who each season purchased three hundred minots of salt for the conservation of his finest stoat, martin and ermine pelts. Henry, whose sole descendant was a nephew, asked to see the child. He envied the Rear-Admiral, he said, after Lily had been presented. How he wished to have even a daughter to whom he could bequeath his worldly goods!

"What would you say to an otter-belly cloak?" he asked the child.

"I don't want one," Lily said. "I only like salt."

That made Alexander Henry smile.

"You are right," he answered. "Armagh salt is more precious than fur. I owe it my life."

Taking her on his knee, he told her how, on June 4, 1763, when he arrived at Fort Michillimakinac, on the south bank of the strait that connects Lake Huron and Lake Michigan, a band of Ojibwas who were camped nearby had come to play ball at the foot of the palisade. There must have been a good hundred of them, fighting with their netted sticks, then scattering in all directions. Suddenly, the ball bounced high in the air and, describing an arc, sailed over the palisade. The guards, not suspecting the stratagem, opened the gates to allow the Indians to retrieve it. They immediately streamed into the fort, shouting war cries. Armed with tomahawks, which their women had hidden beneath their blankets, they began to scalp all the Englishmen they could lay hands on. Because he was not a soldier, Henry escaped that terrible fate. He was captured and sent along with the other prisoners to Beaver Island. In the skirmish, he had taken a tomahawk blow to the arm, and the wound had festered. Had he turned feverish, the Indians would have killed him. Fortunately, in his purse he was carrying Armagh salt. He poured it into the wound, which quickly healed.

"During all the time I spent in the mine," noted Master Anselm, "my wounds never became infected, and yet I do not know how many times I cut my hands."

"Salt has cleansing properties," said Lily. "In times of plague, villages that produced salt were always spared. Irritation from brambles, poison ivy, mosquito bites and bee stings, inflammations of the throat, burns: nothing can resist its action. It can even purify fire. The Devil detests salt because it is incorruptible."

She uncorked her salt flask and threw its contents into the fireplace. The moribund flames suddenly flared to life, crackling and bursting into sparks. In their sudden light, the parlor walls seemed in turn to catch fire. Master Anselm, sensitive to the slightest relief, noted that the stark white surface of those walls was not perfectly smooth, but striated. Their texture, though unusual, brought to mind something familiar. He stretched out his hand to touch it, and encountered a softness into which he would have liked to thrust his hand. The walls were covered with fur!

"Otter-belly fur," noted Lily.

The stone carver had already guessed it. Each bristle he recognized, as though he had sculpted it himself. He attempted to calculate the number of beasts needed to cover the walls. By rough estimate, there must have been a good four hundred.

"I suppose these pelts were purchased from the trader Henry," he said.

"Not all of them," Lily corrected him. "Some of them are from the Loutre. Titus and I fished them out ourselves."

When they were young, she related, they would often abscond from the house to play on the river banks, even if the Rear-Admiral had forbidden it. Yet the Loutre River was not at all dangerous. As wide as it was shallow, it did not so much as flow as let itself be drawn along between the rocks, its surface unbroken by so much as a ripple. One could barely hear its purling. Its waters were the color of rust, and quite clear. One day, however, Lily and Titus, emerging from the path, found themselves face to face with a river whose waters were troubled, almost milky, and that lent a whitish tinge to the alders and spruces that overhung it. Lily discovered the first otter's body, washed ashore on the sandy bank. Titus discovered the second, trapped between two rocks. The current had carried some of them along with it, and others had been caught in the bushes. Moving upstream, the children collected them as they went, until they reached the salt works. It was there that they understood what had caused the otters' death. Huge mounds of salt had been dumped into the river.

"There would have been a fair tonne," said Lily. "When the harvest was too abundant, my father would destroy part of it, to increase the price."

Master Anselm groaned.

"Had he sold his salt less dearly, he would not have needed to protect it so much."

He often saw Magnus McEvoy's caravans pass through Beaumont, he said. Each year they departed Armagh for Quebec City, escorted by never less than six armed men. One recollection stood out in particular: that of the Seigneur of Vincennes, who had been imprudent enough to attack them. This gentleman, Joseph Roy by name, possessed a storage shed on the Beaumont shoreline, where he stored the salt carried by boat from Portachoix or Bargocillau, in Labrador, which he purchased from cod fishermen. He would then re-sell it to Montreal and Quebec City merchants, who could reach him by river. He looked askance at competition from the Irish Rear-Admiral, so he sent a group of hired ruffians against him. The poor wretches returned limping, tails between their legs. From his musket, the Rear-Admiral had fired rock salt at them.

"Do you play the harp?" asked Master Anselm when he saw the diminutive instrument of willow wood standing in a corner of the parlor. Lily indicated that she did not. She had none of the talents in which young ladies were normally instructed. Her education had consisted only of those things related to salt. After all, she said, at Armagh, everything was related to salt. Even the harp. It had been given to the Rear-Admiral by his neighbor Tom Cullen, in gratitude for services rendered.

The two men had met while in the navy, in which Cullen had enlisted at a young age in order to escape his father, a man who could not speak to him without plying his whip. It was only upon his death that Cullen set foot once more in Ireland, and then only to fire the barrels of gunpowder in the ancestral house, it being impossible to demolish with pick and shovel. The only thing he sought to preserve of his inheritance was this Celtic harp, possibly because his father had so loathed music. He brought it with him to Canada and given it pride of place in the parlor of the residence that he had built with the proceeds of the sale of his ancestral lands.

When he established residence in the township, Tom Cullen already had three children, and his wife was expecting a fourth. The kitchen garden of his estate consisted of a salad patch, for his wife, in her state, was a great fancier of green vegetables. From her window she watched them grow, and delighted in seeing them form into heads. "Soon they will be ready to eat!" she exclaimed, one evening.

But on the following morning, when she visited the patch, she found it laid waste. All that remained of the fresh, green leaves were tooth-punctured debris covered with long smears of slime. "Don't touch them," her husband warned her as he rushed up, drawn by her cries. "It's pooka spittle."

Pookas, Lily explained, were a kind of goblin. They assumed different forms and destroyed the crops on isolated farms, and their spittle was said to be extremely poisonous.

To discourage them, Tom Cullen covered his plants and spread wood ash around them. He even left pots of beer lying about, in hopes of intoxicating the malevolent spirits. It was all for naught. Each morning, the tender shoots that had appeared the day before came under attack.

Around that time, Rear-Admiral McEvoy had paid Cullen a visit. He was startled to see his neighbor's wife so thin and pale. "May the pookas be damned," Cullen swore. "I fear she will die if she cannot eat the salad greens from our patch."

The Rear-Admiral, who was not convinced of the truth of those pooka tales, counseled him to dust the soil around his plants with salt—not too much, lest he cause the earth to become barren. His neighbor took his advice. A few days later, the greens began to grow again. On the ground, at their feet, Cullen discovered blackened, curled tongues.

"Salt absorbs not only moisture, but also the humors of snails and slugs," said Lily. "There is no finer way to trap them."

The neighbor made an appearance at Armagh the following Sunday. In an outpouring of gratitude, he had come to make a gift of his harp to his friend. "I have nothing more precious," he said with a certain embarrassment. The Rear-Admiral almost turned him down. "What will we do with a harp that no one knows how to play?" he thought. But when he noticed how fascinated his wife was by the bust of a woman that, like a figure-head on a ship's prow, decorated the column of the harp, he graciously accepted the gift.

Madam McEvoy, who had an ear for music, managed within a few months to learn enough chords to accompany the Rear-Admiral when he sang. The evening parties at the manor became so popular in the township that Magnus McEvoy had the idea of giving a concert in the mine. The place possessed exceptional acoustic qualities which enhanced, more than the parlor, the resonance of each note.

The great central chamber of the mine had been transformed into a festive hall. To reach it, the guests took their places two by two in large wicker baskets. When they reached the bottom, they were welcomed by a thousand lanterns gleaming beneath the shadowed vault. Of their number were several members of the Legislative Council, the widow of the founder of the *Quebec Gazette*, John Montresor, a military engineer with whom the Rear-Admiral had carried out his survey of the Saint Lawrence in 1760, as well as the Chevalier de Niverville, who had been commander of Fort Paskoyac and now directed Indian affairs in Trois-Rivières. Even Governor Carleton, who had just been named Lord Dorchester, granted them the honor of his presence. He was accompanied by his brother Thomas, the hero who had fought the Turks alongside the Russians in 1778. Both were natives of County Tyrone, Northern Ireland. When the sounds of the harp began to reverberate in cadence among the pillars of salt, they broke into tears. At the end of the concert, they could not wait to tell Madam McEvoy how much that crystalline music reminded them of the land of their birth.

It had been Lily's social debut. For the occasion, her mother lent her the gown she had worn on her wedding day. "What finer favor could I do for my daughter?" she exclaimed, magnanimous. But she did not want Perpetuity to make the slightest adjustment, for fear that her needle would leave holes in the silk. The gown was too big for Lily, and too long as well. It was difficult for the girl to walk without tripping over the hem. Besides, she was not in the habit of appearing, especially in front of her father, in such a low-cut bodice. She remained hidden for the entire evening behind one of the salt pillars, licking it from time to time, absent-mindedly. Her mother came looking for her on several occasions, wishing to present her to other young people, encouraging her to come out of her shell, going so far as to pull her by the arm. Lily, on the verge of tears, clutched tight the pillar and refused to move. She would have been more than prepared to dance if only Titus were there! She thought of him, alone in the barn, and her heart swelled with pity.

She placed herself close to the refreshment table, which Father Compain had taken over for two complete hours. When he finally moved on, there remained nary a drop of negus nor of gooseberry wine, and the rice croquettes and potted squirrel had evaporated. The vicar of Beaumont had left a platter of anchovy biscuits untouched, but they seemed to be disappearing from before her very eyes, even though no one approached the table. Just to make sure, Lily counted them twice. She had not been mistaken: no more than twenty biscuits remained, while there had been twenty-three only a short time before. Deciding to keep the table under close scrutiny, after a few moments she saw a hand appear, with supple fingers and dirt beneath the fingernails, and creep confidently toward the plate. She would have recognized that hand anywhere.

She could not help but admire Titus's audacity, while shuddering at the thought of the punishment that awaited him when the Rear-Admiral, who would eventually make his way to the table, discovered him among the guests. That would certainly have been the outcome if the festivities had not suddenly been disrupted by a bloodcurdling cry. All eyes turned in concern toward the entrance to the gallery where the shout had come from. In the general confusion, Lily crawled under the table with Titus. He was lying on his stomach, just as nonchalantly as he would lie in the hay. "Come closer," he whispered. She edged over to his side. She was not worried about soiling her gown, as the floor of the mine was covered with a coating of fine salt. With a finger he lifted the edge of the tablecloth just in time to see the pale, tottering figure of Father Compain emerging from the gallery. He claimed he had wandered into one of the tunnels, but in truth he had ventured there on orders from the bishop, to ascertain the true dimensions of the mine. There, he had encountered the Pawnee Indians. The Indians, as was their custom, had greased and sculpted their hair into the shape of a horn above their foreheads. The vicar thought he had stumbled onto a band of demons.

"That will teach him to stick his nose into other people's business," said Lily. "Next time, he'll stay put in his vicarage."

Titus felt strong affection for the man who had given him his religious education, and he sprang to his defense.

"Why should the Rear-Admiral be the only owner of the mine? Salt is the fruit of the earth. It belongs to everybody."

"You don't know what you're talking about. If my father had not found this vein, no one would have known of its existence. There lies the source of his rights."

"He found me as well. Does that mean I belong to him?"

"He saved you, he took you in. You owe him respect and obedience."

"For how many years? I've had enough of being his servant."

"Patience. After he dies, you will become my personal valet."

"I haven't the slightest intention of being a valet for the rest of my life."

"You shall see, Titus. I will treat you well. You will eat in the kitchen, you will be able to sleep by the hearth, and you will never be beaten."

"Do you think that would be enough to keep me here?"

"I will also pay you, if you desire. And you shall have Easter Sunday as a day off."

"Thank you Lily, but I shall not stay on at Armagh."

"Where will you go?"

"I already told you, the day we visited the processional chapel. To Beaumont, where I will sculpt statues."

"What kind of statues?"

"Statues of saints."

"For Compain, the little vicar?"

"For churches, for convents, for foundling homes."

Around them, in the festive hall, the laughter and conversation seemed to have picked up again as, beneath the table, silence reigned. Propped up on her elbows, Lily began to tremble.

"You will fail," she finally told him, "and you will return to me. I pray God, here and now, for He always grants prayers made to Him in a salt mine."

Titus had drawn close to her and put his arms around her.

"There, there, everything will fine. Don't move. Stay as still as a statue."

She began to weep with rage.

"I won't allow you to be separated from me."

"Then you must follow me."

"You know I'll never leave the estate. When you go, I'll give you Armagh salt. Every night, you must breathe some. If not, you'll forget me."

"I will not. I'll make a bust of you. Just as you are tonight, in your gown that's too big for you."

He drew closer still to her bare throat and placed his lips upon the hollow behind her collarbone, in which Lily's tears had collected.

"Stay close to me," she whispered to him. "In the meantime, I will find a way to keep you."

Her thoughts were interrupted by Perpetuity, who threw open the dining room doors. Master Anselm, standing beside her, seemed equally at a loss for words.

"The soup is served," said the maidservant, discouraged when she saw them shrouded in silence.

"Let us not keep it waiting," Lily responded, beckoning the stone carver with a sweep of her hand to sit down across the table from her.

She felt a shiver of satisfaction when she realized that, of all the objects that had been set upon the table, only the bust sculpted by Titus held his attention. But before he could make mention of it, she motioned to him to begin eating. She noticed that the contents of his plate gave him pause.

"It's a simple broth of wild roots," she said. "One of my mother's recipes, who got it from her own mother."

Laurence McEvoy, Lily revealed to Master Anselm, had always claimed to be an orphan. But in truth she was the illegitimate child of one of the young seigneurs whose estates lined the banks of the river. That man, whose name she had never been able to discover, apparently had a reputation as a free thinker, a blasphemer and a rake, particularly among the serving maids of the house. One day, a virtuous cook's apprentice caught his eye. He contrived to seduce her with the promise of a gold ring, a rather slender ring at that. She was Laurence's mother. In short order he impregnated her but, having become attached to her, he was reluctant to disavow her. Before his father got wind of the affair, he sent her to one of the islands in the River, where his family owned land. There she could hide her disgrace. But at least he'd been charitable enough to settle her in a hut and give her geese to tend.

Some time later, the former cook gave birth to a girl, with the rushing of the river as her only companion. That was why she baptized the child Laurence. As the years went by, with the greatest difficulty the two of them managed to subsist on the island, for they were entitled to kill only one goose per season. They fed themselves on herring and eel, which they caught in pots. Often, in exchange for a few morsels of meat, they would help the sealers butcher their catch. Along the shore they would gather whatever could be eaten, from algae and shellfish to salt grasses. By dint of walking barefoot in the mud, their feet had become deformed.

Their primitive life would undoubtedly have followed its course had the British not dropped anchor off the island in June of 1760. They had come to sound the river bottom in that particular place, and to study the fluctuations of the currents and the tides. Upon spying the foreign flag, the mother fled in terror to hide in the hut, abandoning her child on the shore. Laurence stood there alone as the majestic frigate hove to. She, who at ten years of age, had never seen anything larger than a fishing boat, was captivated by the spectacle of the *Galatea*—for it was indeed the ship of Magnus McEvoy. But it had not been its sixty cannons, nor its sails nor its rigging that had drawn her admiration, but the sculpted figure that graced its prow.

"A figurehead!" exclaimed Master Anselm, his eyes half closed. "Representing what? A lion? A unicorn? A winged victory?"

"A woman's bust, and no more," said Lily. "She must have been very beautiful because, according to my father, the members of the crew would sometimes fall in love with her during their long voyages at sea."

"That does not surprise me. Statues have the power to beguile that no portrait possesses. All the more so, since figureheads have no rival in sight."

Lily dismissed his claim impatiently. She ill-fancied figureheads. They always stared straight ahead, as if what they left behind in their wake was not worthy of consideration. If it had been up to her, she once declared to her father, ships would display such figures astern.

Laurence, she continued, was entranced by the sight of Magnus McEvoy when he appeared on the frigate's forecastle.

At thirty-three, he was still only a captain, but he had a proud look about him, with his cocked hat and his blue greatcoat with white lapels. While the men busied themselves casting their leads, he climbed over the rail where, suspended from the bowsprit, he hung for a considerable time in contemplation of the figurehead. When Laurence beheld the spectacle, she cried out in distress. For the first time in her existence, she felt the most dire of all cravings—the one that, blinded by the attraction of another person, inspires only self-loathing. In her desire to resemble the figurehead, she threw back her head and thrust her chest forward. From high upon the bridge, the captain had not even noticed her, too busy giving the order to make sail. "No matter," she said to herself as she watched the frigate stand off from the shore. "One day, I shall be as beautiful as the statue on that ship."

"That was how my parents' destinies met for the first time," said Lily as she rang for Perpetuity to bring the rest of the meal.

Then noticing the soup plate that Master Anselm had barely touched, she asked, "Are you not going to finish your broth? Perhaps my conversation has made it difficult for you to swallow."

"I never eat such salty fare, your Excellency."

"You are wrong. Food can never be too salty. Just think, Master Anselm! Salt is the only edible mineral. It is also, they say, the fifth element. Unlike sugar or spices, it is essential to human life, and to the lives of animals as well. Deprive yourself of salt for one day and your head will begin to spin. After one week, you will feel nauseous. After one month, you will die."

Taking a platter of anchovies and herring in brine from Perpetuity, she offered them to her guest. After all that she had said, he thought it better to help himself to a generous portion.

"My father taught me early on to salt everything, even tea. Sugar, he liked to say, is for weaklings. By weaklings, he meant the French, of course."

"Here at Armagh, you have salt in abundance. Elsewhere, it is costly, and must be consumed sparingly."

"Not as expensive as in Timbuktu, where it is worth its weight in gold, so they say."

"The salt of Armagh has certainly made a fortune for the McEvoys."

"Salt is not rare, Master Anselm, but to harvest it is an arduous task. Rock salt must be extracted from the ground, most often at great depths. Salt springs require, for crystallization, immense boilers and the wood of entire forests. Sea salt can only be harvested after spending weeks in evaporating basins in the marshes. So much effort for so little result. That is what has always justified its high price."

The ancients, she continued, attributed such value to salt that they used it as a medium of exchange. The Romans used it to pay their soldiers, and the Egyptians, to embalm their mummies. The salt trade gave Venice its supremacy over Genoa in the Mediterranean. It filled the privy purse of the kings of Poland, the coffers of the Hapsburgs and the pockets of the ship owners of Liverpool; it made the herring and cod fishery such a lucrative one. We should not be surprised to learn that salt has caused more wars than gold.

"Besides," she concluded peremptorily, "had the King of France not taxed it so highly, his subjects would not have revolted."

Master Anselm swallowed the last of his anchovies. His throat was parched, and he wished for nothing more than a drink of water. But there were neither glasses nor carafes on the table. With his fork, he crushed a grain of salt that had remained on the edge of his plate.

"How can something so small be such a source of discord?"

"Not only of discord," Lily protested. "To eat salt with someone is to seal a pact of friendship. Remember God's words, when he contracted His covenant with mankind."

"I don't believe I know about that."

"God decreed that salt henceforth be cast upon all burnt offerings. For salt, which has the power to conserve, is the guarantor of an indissoluble alliance. My parents also contracted a covenant of salt of a kind. My father provided it, and my mother found new uses for it."

"How many uses can salt possibly have?" asked Master Anselm. Every time Lily mentioned Laurence, his irritation grew sharper.

"Exactly four thousand," Lily answered, with perfect seriousness.

By way of example, she explained that the tapers in the candelabrum burned but did not melt because they had been soaked for two hours in salt water. Master Anselm nodded. She took that as her signal to continue.

"What can they possibly be doing?" asked Ursula when Perpetuity finally returned from the dining room.

"They're talking about candelabra and salt water."

"Ha, the festivities are off to a fine start!"

"The evening is still young. Much can still happen."

"How do you expect them to speak intimate words when they don't even have wine to loosen their tongues?"

"In the days when the Rear-Admiral and Madam McEvoy had dinner parties, they were gay affairs. They spent most of their time titillating each other. And when they weren't making eyes, they'd be playing footsie under the table. How many times did I catch her sitting on his lap, whispering sweet nothings in his ear? And he would purr like a cat. The presence of the child didn't bother them. Sometimes I was ashamed for them.

"Is Lily smiling at Master Anselm?"

"No."

"Looking him in the eye?"

"Neither."

"Salt is all she talks about! You can see she has no designs on him. Besides, you said so yourself. He's not the man he was ten years ago."

"All I said was that his skin seems tanned by salt. As far as he's concerned, believe you me, he still has the full vigor of his youth."

"Come now, Perpetuity, stop dreaming. Lily has no intention of marrying, and we won't be given permission any day soon to bring sugar into this house."

"Then why this dinner? Admit it, Her Excellency is cooking something up."

"If that's so, she's not the only one. Titus came by just five minutes ago. He didn't want his bowl. He took some bread and dried meat and stuffed them into his haversack. It looked as though he was in a rush."

Perpetuity lifted her finger and motioned for them to listen.

"I hear Her Excellency ringing."

"Quick, take this ham and slice it!"

"The meat is all shriveled up. Didn't you boil it?"

133

"Of course not, I roasted it on the spit. Lily was worried it would lose its salt."

"And she's going to serve this to Master Anselm? The poor devil, he'll die of thirst."

Despite Ursula's convincing arguments, Perpetuity had not given up the hope that, when she entered the dining room, Lily and her guest would have drawn closer together, that they might even have entwined their fingers in the center of the table. She was distressed to discover that they had not so much as moved from their places, and that they were still seated as stiffly as before. She deposited the platters of bear ham, smoked partridge and pickled salicorne on the table, then returned to the kitchen, discouraged. If she had tarried only a few moments longer, she would have had the pleasure of seeing Lily rise from her armchair, walk around the table and bend over Master Anselm's shoulder.

"If you please," she said. "Allow me to offer you some salt."

One by one, she opened the nineteen salt cellars. Each one contained, she explained, salts of different origins. She insisted that he taste of each from the tip of a knife, for to touch it with one's fingers brought bad luck. Master Anselm hesitated before the different crystals that ranged from white to dark gray, which were tinged pink or yellow, depending on whether they contained algae, clay or sulfur.

"Which one should I begin with?" he asked.

First, Lily presented him with the sea salts, crystallized in marshes in which sea water, as it evaporates, turns red; those of Alexandria, Cyprus, Crete and Trapani, particularly prized for having been mentioned in the writings of Pliny; that of the Camargue, drawn as well from the Mediterranean; the white salt of Setubal, in Portugal, and the gray salt of Noirmoutier, both harvested along the shores of the Atlantic; that of the fabulous Dead Sea with its viscous waters, and of the Indian Ocean, where it was gathered by blind workers; the salt of the North Sea, which is harvested from peat ash; and finally, the black salt of the volcanic islands of Hawaii, a gift sent to the Rear-Admiral by his old friend, Captain Cook.

"It takes four hundred gallons of sea water to produce a single bushel of salt," she pointed out.

Then came the rock salts of the Wieliczka mine in Poland, and the Muntaya de Sal in Cardona, Spain. They had been preserved in the most opaque of the salt cellars, for were they exposed to light, they would lose their salinity. Finally, there were the salts from the deposits at Salzburg and Halle, from Salies-de-Béarn, and from Kanawha in Virginia, and from Salsomaggiore, which were reserved for the manufacture of Parma ham.

"The quicker the evaporation," Lily explained, "the finer the grains of salt. Still, not even the salt pans with the most rapid rate of evaporation can ever produce a salt to match ours in fineness."

It could not be denied, she went on, that Armagh salt was the most precious of them all. And so it was kept in the most handsome of all the salt cellars, a bark carved from hematite upon which one could make out, in relief, the image of the *Galatea*, the frigate once commanded by the Rear-Admiral. It had been placed directly in front of Master Anselm, as befitted the guest of honor. Clearly, said Lily, it could not be compared with the agate cellar belonging to the Duc de Berry, with its gold, sapphire and pearl-encrusted cover, or the one created by Benvenuto Cellini, fitted with drawers for pepper and antidote powders. Still, its details had been sculpted with great delicacy, she asserted, turning suddenly to Master Anselm.

"But I am telling you nothing new. You know this salt cellar better than anyone else ..."

The stone carver let the cover drop with a sharp thud.

"This one and all the others. You never forget the work to which you devote so much attention."

"My father must have paid you handsomely for you to agree to part with them."

"You are wrong. These salt cellars meant nothing to me. I carved them for him. Every year I gave him one, from his wedding day until his death. I asked nothing in exchange, and he gave me nothing. Not even a word of thanks. So says Father Compain, who acted as my intermediary."

"Why did you continue with your generosity?"

Master Anselm took time to swallow before answering. His mouth was dry as a bone. He thought Lily would offer him something to drink. But she did no such thing.

When his father died, he finally said, he wanted to return to work for Monsignor Briand. But the bishop, who had promised to re-engage him in his service, did not keep his word. He let him to languish in Beaumont, and ordered only small pieces on rare occasions. One of those trinkets, a salt flask carved in amethyst, nonetheless gave him the idea of creating a salt cellar expressly for Magnus McEvoy in hopes of dazzling him, and flattering him so he would agree to become his new protector. Upon completing the work, he departed for Armagh with the relief of the *Argo* under his arm. But when he presented himself at the main gate

136

of the estate, the Rear-Admiral refused to receive him. He had to entrust his gift to the agency of Father Compain, who upon his return related how the Rear-Admiral had accepted the object without a word. Master Anselm did not give in to discouragement. The following year he tried once more with a salt cellar in serpentine upon which one could admire the silhouette of the *Petite Hermine*. He never received a response. Over time, his annual offering became an occasion to ridicule the Rear-Admiral for his silence. Then it turned into nothing more than the proof of his stubbornness.

"Do you know why my father refused to see you?" asked Lily.

"I was not certain."

"But did you not suspect something?"

"The mind must make suppositions when it receives no answer," he said. "Who can endure silence? I thought he was challenging me to do better. But when I entered this room, I understood why your father so callously ignored me." Picking up the bust that Lily had placed in the center of the table, he declared in a broken voice, "It is clear that he found a craftsman more capable than myself."

Lily leaned toward him.

"Do you really believe that this salt cellar is comparable to yours?" she whispered.

"I have never done anything but bas-relief. This bust required a talent greater than mine."

A look of delight spread over Lily's face.

"A remarkable talent … That is my view as well. But in my opinion, you underestimate your own."

Faced with Titus's work, Master Anselm felt humbled. He preferred to change the subject.

"I have been talking too much, my throat is dry. Would you be so kind as to bring me some water?"

"I shall ring for Perpetuity in a moment. First, I would like you to taste this," she said, pointing to the salt that had collected in the two hollows of the bust's collarbones.

Master Anselm thrust his knifepoint into the deposit. After having smelled the white powder, he deposited a bit upon his tongue, and immediately felt a burning sensation.

"You have spilled some," noted Lily. "This portends no good."

"This salt is bitter," said the stone carver.

"How could it be anything else? This is the salt that, over the years, I have collected from the evaporation of my tears. Its bitterness, Master Anselm, is the taste of resentment."

"Do you not think," said Lily, returning to her seat across the table from her guest, "that, of all our emotions, resentment is the only one that derives from an act of will? Fear and surprise, joy and sadness, affection and hatred, anger and shame: we experience the upheavals they bring without being able to do anything about them. Can the heart be kept from loving? From hating? He who attempts to stifle his jealousy or overcome his antipathies will quickly understand how futile such an enterprise is."

"Don't you think that resentment has the same dominion over us?" asked Master Anselm.

"It is a state into which we decide to place ourselves, by consciously refusing to pardon a wrong or an offense. We must work to maintain ourselves in that state, by constantly returning to the slight, long after it has occurred."

"It is not necessary to be the victim of a slight to experience the emotion."

"Certainly not. Resentment is all the more intense when one's family or ancestors have been slighted. And even should one inadvertently wipe the slate clean, it loses nothing of its essence. It is enough to invoke a single painful memory and it leaps once more to life, more tenacious than ever. In this regard, it quite resembles salt, which, even having been diluted, will form crystals anew with the first evaporation."

"Resentment is foreign to me," said Master Anselm, "for my memory is weak. I am inclined to drown the past in forgetfulness. But you speak of it as something that must be preserved."

"Perhaps because I have dedicated the last ten years to keeping mine alive."

"You! I am unaware that you have had such enmity. Toward whom have you nourished such feelings?"

Lily smiled with her pointed teeth. With a serpent's hiss, she answered, "Toward you, Master Anselm. Is that not clear enough?"

In the dining room, the tapers had almost burned down to the nub. Lily intended to ring for Perpetuity to replace them, but the stone carver, who had forgotten his thirst, restrained her.

"Tell me, first of all, in what manner have I offended you?"

Before answering, Lily ran her finger over the bust.

"Salt also preserves the memory of old wrongs," she said. "Those which you inflicted upon my family go far back indeed."

Ensconced in her armchair, she described how her mother had come to Armagh on a stormy night in October 1770. The Rear-Admiral found her at the manor door, huddled in an old sealskin cloak. He quickly invited her in, and begged her to take a seat in front of the fire. She moved aside, better to make room for him. They gazed at one another in silence, unable to believe their good fortune.

"You see," Lily explained, "both of them had been waiting for this reunion ever since they met at Beaumont."

That day, when he saw Laurence in Master Anselm's workshop, the Rear-Admiral was dumbfounded. He pretended to be struck by her resemblance with the altarpiece in the chapel of Our Lady of the River. But his emotion arose from an entirely different source. The way she lifted her head and thrust forward her bosom—she was exactly like the beloved lost figurehead of his former frigate. His thoughts returned to her with longing, as an incarnation of what is most confident and yet most disconcerting about a woman. He was amazed to learn that the girl, far from being the head of the household, was being kept in a state of servitude.

"So you know that Laurence worked in my house," the stone carver interrupted.

"I found out by listening behind closed doors, since my parents made every effort to conceal that fact. I overheard bits of their conversation, pieced them together with the secrets the maidservants used to trade, and I have come to reconstitute the whole story. The story in which your name would constantly recur, Master Anselm."

"Do me the favor, then, of satisfying my curiosity. It was well known that Magnus McEvoy kept the gate of his estate closed tight. How did Laurence manage to enter?"

"She had the key."

"And where did she get it?"

"My father handed it to her. Right under your nose."

The Rear-Admiral, continued Lily, was so taken with Laurence that he would have abducted her then and there, but he dared not believe he might please her. After all, he was twenty-three years older than her—and he was by no means as handsome a man as Master Anselm, who he assumed was his rival. He employed a subterfuge, and slipped the key to the estate into a pouch of salt, which he offered the girl, with the recommendation that she use it as she saw fit.

"Why all the concealment?" asked Master Anselm, shaking his head. "If the Rear-Admiral had asked to have my maidservant, I would have gladly handed her over to him, on the condition that he grant me a commission ..."

"My father desired that she come to him of her own accord."

By the hearth at Armagh, Laurence told the Rear-Admiral how moved she was to rediscover the captain whom she had sighted on the prow of his frigate. He told her how he regretted ignoring that child on the shore. The following morning he departed for Quebec City, begging Laurence to wait for him at the manor. He returned ten days later, announcing that he had returned to the religion of his forefathers and that, at the cathedral, the bans had been published. For his fiancée, he brought two maidservants, as well as a white gown and cloak made of otter-belly fur.

"I remember that cloak," said Anselm. "I saw Laurence wearing it on her wedding day."

"Do you think that your hateful presence at the main gate escaped her attention? She was so appalled that she didn't have the strength to ask my father to have you driven away. She was left with the premonition that you would be the cause of all her persecutions. And, in fact, the first was soon to come."

A scant month had elapsed since the wedding ceremony, explained Lily, when Madam McEvoy began suffering from indispositions. She confided in Perpetuity, who told her how delighted she was that she would soon become a mother, but how startled she was that the blessed event had occurred so precipitously. Her comment planted a seed of doubt in the mind of the young bride as to who the father was. She did not dare appear in front of the Rear-Admiral until she was quite certain; she locked herself in the turret for the entire gestation period. The day of her deliverance, which fell eight lunations later, confirmed her worst fears.

"The child whom she brought into the world was among your works, Master Anselm," Lily declared. "What say you to that?"

The stone carver's eyes suddenly glistened.

"Lily, why would you have waited ten years to reveal this to me? Why deprive me of the relief that this unexpected news brings me?"

"What ill has been weighing so heavily on you?"

"The fear of dying without posterity."

"These salt cellars carved by your hand are not sufficient notice of your passage here below?"

"Surely. But who, one day, will pay their respects before my mortal remains? Only a child can properly honor the memory of his parents, as you have so proven in the mine. Oh! Fear not! I am not hard to please, and I ask of you nothing so grand. A simple cross in the Beaumont cemetery would be more than enough. And, were it not too much to ask, a mass, once a year."

"Why should I have Mass sung for you?"

"So that my soul will find rest. The resentment you bear me cannot keep you from discharging your filial duty."

Lily burst into laughter.

"My filial duty! How dare you take me for your daughter? I am the faithful portrait of my father."

Master Anselm drew back in anger.

"Then what is the purpose of this charade?"

"Come now, think! If we consider the number of salt cellars, your child would have been nineteen when my father died. He would be twenty-nine today. Whereas I am only twenty-seven."

The stone carver had to make the calculation several times over. A splitting headache aggravated by thirst had addled his mind, and now emotion increased his confusion. He finally came around to Lily's opinion. Almost thirty years had elapsed since his encounter with Laurence.

"You had a son, Master Anselm," Lily said with a sneer that revealed all the hatred of her rancorous soul. "Would you like to know what he has become?"

Anselm did not answer.

After recovering from childbirth in the solitude of the turret, Lily related, Madam McEvoy wondered what she would do with the infant she had unfortunately brought into the world. She did not want to keep it, but she could not simply cast it into the Loutre. One thing was certain. She could not present him to the Rear-Admiral before a month had elapsed. She kept it hidden in her bedchamber, taking care to clutch it tight to her breast to prevent it from crying.

With the first new moon of 1772, she placed the infant in his cradle and sent Perpetuity to summon her husband. The Rear-Admiral, who had not seen his spouse since the preceding autumn, hastened to her bedside. He found her sitting up in bed, admirably disposed. He kissed her, then went to the cradle to see his son.

Magnus McEvoy had little experience with newborns. He would have suspected nothing had not Perpetuity, who had seen more than a few at the foundling home, expressed surprise that the child's navel was already showing a scar, whereas normally the umbilical cord took three full weeks to dry up before dropping off. Magnus McEvoy turned immediately to his spouse.

With perfect self-control, she cried out, "No cord? You are mistaken. He had it just a few moments ago!"

"See for yourself," said Perpetuity, holding up the nursling.

Madam McEvoy began to wring her hands in lamentation.

"Woe is me! This is not our son! Jealous fairies must have stolen him away, and replaced him with this changeling while I slept."

She moved to her husband's side, her head held high, her bosom thrust forward, in that attitude both confident and disquieting that always melted his hard resolve. The Rear-Admiral looked her straight in the eye and smiled a knowing smile. In Ireland, he had often heard tell of children being stolen by fairies. Though he believed neither in the one nor the other, he declared, "There is only one way to determine whether the child is a changeling, and that's to baptize it."

In case of dire necessity, he added, a father is entitled to perform the sacramental rite in the place of the vicar.

"Your Excellency," Perpetuity interrupted, "are you in a state of grace?"

"Bring me some water and salt. In the meantime, I shall induce myself into the most perfect possible contrition."

When Perpetuity returned, he breathed lightly on the newborn's face. Then he made the sign of the cross over his forehead and his heart, stretched his right hand over him and placed a few grains of holy salt in his mouth. The infant frowned and began to cry.

"He does not like salt," the Rear-Admiral declared. "He can be no son of mine." Turning to his wife, he told her, "Forget this child. You will never see it again. But be consoled, for we shall soon have another heir."

Madam McEvoy understood that their covenant, this covenant of salt that together they had contracted, was indissoluble. And as for that changeling the Rear-Admiral baptized Titus, it was sent off to a wet nurse the very next day.

When he heard the name Titus, Master Anselm took his head in his hands and damned Magnus McEvoy.

"Why didn't he return my son to me instead of making him his valet?"

Lily sighed.

"That's what you say now. But yesterday, would you have taken him in?"

She had grown up, she said, convinced that her father was keeping a wild child in a cage. That was how the Rear-Admiral explained the cries that could be heard, on stormy nights, coming from the stable. To frighten her, he told her that the child, if this malignant creature could be called that, had been trapped in the mine, where he had been drawn by the smell of salt. It had taken four Pawnees to overcome him, so desperately had he struggled. One of them, his flesh torn by his venomous black claws, almost died of his wounds.

Lily imagined the child had a wolf's features, or sometimes, those of a badger. At night, she thought she could hear him scratching at her window with his poisonous claws. Every time she heard the noise of Ursula slaughtering a capon, she hoped it was the wild child being killed.

Yet she kept prowling around the stable, which her father had forbidden her to do. Sometimes she would creep up to one of the windows and stand on tiptoe, then flee as fast as her legs could carry her, since she lacked the courage to look inside.

As she grew older, her fascination finally overcame her fear. One day—she must have been seven years old, for she no longer wore a smock—while her parents were locked in their room exchanging sweet nothings, she entered the stable. The animals were in the fields, the mangers were empty, yet wisps of straw swirled through the air in golden eddies. Something was hiding in the shadows, a presence that seemed more mysterious than threatening. Emboldened by the little knife she had taken pains to arm herself with, she moved forward with furtive steps to the watering trough. Just then, the little boy leaped out at her.

He was sturdy, with frightened eyes and dark skin, and was dressed in rags that showed the scars of animal horns. She retreated, fearing he would show his claws. But the child could not have hurt a flea. His hands were encased in two eviscerated cattle hooves, attached to his arms with tight harnesses.

"You're Lily," he said.

146

The gentle tone of his voice touched her. She did not think that he would know how to speak.

"How do you know?" she answered.

"From Ursula. Every morning and night, she brings me my bowl. Sometimes Perpetuity comes with her, and they tell me about the manor."

"Are you the wild child?"

"Titus is my name. As far as I can remember, I've always been a stable boy. I change the litter, fill the racks and give the animals their salt. There's nothing better to give them an appetite."

"You never go outside?"

"His Excellency forbids it. On Sunday, when you are at Mass, I disobey. I run as far as the river and I don't come back till night."

Lily looked wide-eyed at the boy who dared challenge her father's orders.

"Who put hooves on your hands?"

"His Excellency. So that I don't touch anything."

The Rear-Admiral, he explained, was trying to correct his bad habit of running his hands over everything to learn about its form. Titus had noticed that the natural world, aside from that part of it that was liquid, was entirely constituted of humps and hollows.

"Me too?" Lily asked.

"I think so. But I cannot be positive unless I can see for myself."

Lily didn't know what to think about this provocation.

"If I take off your hooves, will you promise not to scratch me?"

"You have nothing to fear. Every week, Ursula cuts my nails short. If she didn't, they would make holes in my hands. Will you swear not to say anything to your father?"

He spat on the ground and she, mightily impressed, imitated him. Then she turned her attention to the harnesses, which took her an eternity to untie, so tightly were they knotted. Choking back a cry of pain, Titus opened his hands. Often, he said, his fingers were so numb that he had to pry them apart with his teeth.

"Well?" said Lily impatiently as he ran his stiff hands across her face.

Titus didn't seem to hear her. She pulled his hair.

"Well, do I have bumps and hollows?" she cried.

"I don't know," he answered, his eyes suddenly brimming with tears. "All I can feel is sweetness."

"Is that what's making you sad?"

"I've never touched anyone before."

"Don't dry your tears," she said, keeping him from using his handkerchief. "Let me do it."

Slumped deep in his chair, Master Anselm seemed to be on the verge of sobs as well.

"Cattle hooves!" he repeated. "Has anyone ever beheld such cruelty? And you hold resentment against me ... Between he who engenders a son and he who mistreats him, who is the guiltier?"

"My father was simply attempting to correct what you had transmitted to Titus."

"And what might that be?"

"His curiosity for the shape of things."

"Is that such a great fault?"

"Yes, if it is accompanied by the desire to give shape to matter, which is incompatible with the farmhand's station. Don't forget that my father was, for a time, rewarded for his diligence."

148

Titus, she continued, had been so well trained to keep his fists clenched that he soon no longer needed his hooves. He was given permission to accompany the beasts to the fields. He also took over the reins of the carriage when the Rear-Admiral began to suffer from gout. He was free to move about, as long as he did not approach the manor or its inhabitants. Under no circumstances was he to appear before Madam McEvoy. Whenever she prepared to go out, one of the maidservants would ring a bell. When he heard it, Titus was under orders to hide in the barn.

Alas, curiosity finally overcame obedience. The farmhand, drawn like a peppered moth by the lights of the manor, took up a position beneath the windows of the parlor, one evening when a festive reception was underway, and Madam McEvoy had the misfortune of catching a glimpse of him. She had not seen her son since the day of their separation, but she recognized him beyond the shadow of a doubt. This encounter with the fruit of her sin threw her into such disarray that she fell ill. She rejected her husband's assistance and turned to Father Compain. She asked to confess then and there. Lily had no trouble conveying to Master Anselm the exact content of her mother's revelations to the priest in the secrecy of her chambers. The reason was simple: Lily had heard the conversation through a listening hole in the trap door. Madam McEvoy admitted Titus's origins, and expressed the anguish that brought her to detest the sin she had committed so long ago. She asked nothing better than to gain pardon through expiation. As penitence, the vicar advised her to build a chapel on the Armagh road, and to entrust him with the boy's education, for he had lived too long without the benefit of religion. From now on, he suggested, each time the boy would go to grind the grain at the Beaumont mill, he would stop off at the vicarage to hear a page or two of Holy Writ.

Father Compain was quickly taken by Titus. The boy's happy disposition never seemed to falter, except when his condition as a foundling was mentioned. The vicar, held to a vow of silence by the seal of the sacrament, regretted not being able to reveal to him his father's identity. But he nonetheless decided to bring them together, if ever so slightly. He did more than edify his pupil; he took him to pray at the Beaumont processional chapel.

"That's where the Our Lady of the River altarpiece is," said Master Anselm. "Titus must have drawn great consolation from it."

"So you think!" said Lily in disgust. "As soon as he saw it, he forgot what he had been trained for. He could not resist the temptation to pull his hands from his pockets and touch it. And that was to turn his head."

Indeed, no sooner had he run his fingers over the slate relief than he began deploring his status as a farmhand, and talking of leaving Armagh one day to do something with his hands. Nothing else would matter, as long as he could make sculptures like this one. He wanted to know who had executed it. Father Compain told him of a certain Master Anselm, who lived at the edge of the cliff and knew all the secrets of stone carving. This craftsman, he confirmed, was seeking an apprentice.

"I never did find one," said Master Anselm faintly.

"Would you have taken Titus in had he knocked on your door?" asked Lily.

"What does it matter, since he did not?"

"Humility restrained him. He did not believe himself worthy of receiving your instruction."

Father Compain, meanwhile, remained unswerving in his resolution.

"That year," she said, "instead of delivering the new salt cellar that you had given my father, he entrusted the commission to Titus. He was sure that by allowing the lad to hold one of your works in his hands long enough, he would achieve his ends more rapidly."

The farmhand was in no hurry. His humility exceeded only by his pride, he wanted, before becoming an apprentice, to surpass the master. From age sixteen to nineteen, while he devoted himself to carving stone in the secrecy of the barn, he acted as a messenger for Father Compain on four occasions. That way, he was able to appreciate the carved reliefs of the *Argo*, the *Grande Hermine*, the *Batavia*, but none of them had such an effect on him as the last of the lot—the representation of a frigate of the British fleet.

The *Galatea* is indeed my finest piece," murmured Master Anselm, caressing it with his eyes.

"That was my father's opinion when Titus brought it to him. He quickly realized just how mistaken he was."

The day after that salt cellar arrived, Madam McEvoy had to take to her bed, laid low by a raging fever that carried her away in a night. Of fragile constitution, she had never entirely recovered from the unexpected encounter with Titus, four years earlier. For all her daily devotions in the Armagh chapel, she remained prone to bouts of melancholy. This time, however, she was racked by nightmares that lessened only as she slipped into delirium.

The Rear-Admiral was beside himself, and could not bear to leave her bedside. He kept watch over her poor body that he had so venerated, and that now lay, wrought by convulsions, beneath the bed covers. With dawn came treacherous hope. Calmer now, Madam McEvoy opened her eyes and looked at her husband, though she barely seemed able to see him. Her lips spoke inaudible words, always the same words, whose meaning the Rear-Admiral desperately tried to grasp, with his hand cupping his ear. "The salt cellar ..." he thought she said, then his wife breathed her last.

When he came to awaken Lily to bring her the sad news, he was crushed. Laurence, for him, had been the salt of the earth. Without her, everything had lost its taste, even the salt of Armagh. He was sure that he would not outlive her long. So he decided not to bury her immediately, but to keep her close to him, in the mine. "The salt will preserve her until I can join her," he declared.

Once he had salted his wife's body, the last words she uttered came back to haunt him, said Lily. At first, he tried to forget them, but since they left him no respite, he yielded, and came downstairs to the dining room in the dark of night.

With the upset of the previous days, no one had thought to put away the salt cellar, which had been left in the middle of the table. The Rear-Admiral put on his eyeglasses to examine its decoration. Upon seeing the ship's prow, he understood what had caused the demise of the woman he had so adored.

Lily took a deep breath, and pointed an accusatory finger at the salt cellar.

"The resentment that drove you to create this poisoned gift must have been deep indeed."

"My finest salt cellar!" exclaimed Master Anselm, outraged. "What is poisonous about it?"

"Have you forgotten the figurehead? You must have known my mother would be shattered when she saw that you represented her with a skull ..."

Master Anselm put on an offended look.

"A skull is but an ornament. How could I have imagined that Laurence would think it was intended for her? To hear you, one would think I created that salt cellar with murderous intent."

"Admit that you were burning for revenge."

"Revenge for what? Laurence abandoned me, Magnus McEvoy ignored me, so be it. But I had long since pardoned them. I am not like you, Lily. I am not a man of resentment."

"The water that has flowed under the bridge since those days must have diluted your conscience. Or perhaps you are simply not the kind of man to admit your misdeeds."

"And even if I were to admit them? What is done is done, and cannot be undone, nor redone. Believe me, it's far better to think only of the morrow."

"Every wave must recede after having broken, and the ebb is often stronger than the flow. No one can escape it. Dissolution awaits those who do not reexamine their past, Master Anselm. Salt, fortunately, allows us to confront it."

"I have had quite enough of your resentment, Your Excellency, and thirst torments me. Permit me now to drink."

He made as if to get up from his chair. A gesture from Lily stopped him.

"Suffer a little longer, and be patient," she said, "for I have not yet revealed to you the cause of my resentment."

The Rear-Admiral, she continued when Master Anselm was fully seated, let out a cry of rage when he discovered the figurehead's macabre face. His first impulse was to run to the stone carver's to seek an accounting and obtain satisfaction. Impatient to set out, he took his greatcoat and, lantern in hand, hastened to the barn to awaken Titus. He found him wrapped in a blanket at the foot of a haystack.

"Get dressed and harness the horses," he ordered him after shaking him awake. "You will be driving me to Beaumont tonight."

Titus obeyed unquestioningly. While he was in the stable, the Rear-Admiral waited in the barn. He was shaking with anger, and the pains of gout had begun to torment his foot. Still, he strode back and forth from one corner of the hayloft to the other, throwing aside the pitchforks, kicking the hay, displacing sacks of oats. So it was that Magnus McEvoy discovered, between the folds of a tarpaulin, what should have remained hidden.

"What was under the tarpaulin?" asked Master Anselm, who was burning to get it over with as quickly as possible.

"It was a bust—the same bust you see before you. It gleamed in the light of the lantern just as it gleams now, with the most life-like brilliance, taunting my father."

"How could a simple farmhand have possessed such a jewel?"

"Your lack of perspicacity is all the more dismal when you consider that the person we are speaking of is your son, dear Master. Titus had sculpted it himself from a block of salt, with the little knife he used to castrate chicks."

Master Anselm stared at the bust and rubbed his head.

"Titus? Titus sculpted this?"

"Yes. Titus not only inherited your quirks, but your gifts. My father understood immediately."

The Rear-Admiral, she went on, was by then blind with fury. He realized that his efforts to destroy all traces of the father in the son had been for naught. Abandoning his plan to punish the hand that had fashioned the lethal salt cellar, he turned on his offspring. He seized Titus by the collar and, gout-ridden though he was, dragged him to the Loutre River.

"My father pushed him into the salt works and tied his hands to the millstone. Then he threw open the millrace and the paddlewheel began to turn. Almost immediately, the heavy piles were raised up with a deafening noise. As they fell, Titus's hands were crushed beneath their latticed steel plates."

Master Anselm felt nauseous. He turned pale and closed his eyes. Lily seized on his moment of weakness to undo her purse strings. She was about to remove her amethyst vial when the stone carver began to speak.

"If anyone deserves your resentment," he said, "it is your father and not I, who played only an indirect role in the whole affair."

"Quite the opposite! My father will always have my gratitude. Had he not taken prompt action, Titus would surely have left Armagh ten years ago. While you ..."

"Will you finally tell me what I have done to you?"

Lily re-knotted her purse strings.

"You forced me," she declared, "to betray my half-brother. How could I ever forgive you?"

The last candles in the dining room candelabrum were about to flicker out. Lily hurried to conclude.

Her father had always maintained that if a girl eats salt before going to bed, her future husband will appear in her dreams, bringing water to quench her thirst. She never wanted to put herself to the test, for the simple reason that she did not wish to find a husband. It was enough for Titus to remain her valet.

"When he began to talk of statues," she continued, "I made fun of him. But the day I saw this bust of salt, I realized he would leave, and that I could not keep him."

Even her mother's death a short time later had not caused her as much grief as the thought of losing Titus, she confessed. She was mourning his imminent departure the night her father's shouts awoke her. She rushed downstairs to the dining room, and found the Rear-Admiral in tears, seated in front of the salt cellar.

"Anselm will pay for this," he said, showing Lily the figurehead with the skull. "I shall break his hands with stones, and his blood will flow as far as Armagh."

His words gave Lily a way to keep Titus.

She went to her father's side. What if Anselm were not the guilty party? she had suggested. A stone carver of his reputation would never allow himself such a practical joke. No, Titus should be the object of his suspicion. He brought the salt cellar at the behest of Father Compain. He would have had the opportunity to gouge out the figurehead's eyes, and transform its face into a death's head.

"Why would Titus do such a thing?" the Rear-Admiral asked.

"Out of envy, for all he dreams of is surpassing Master Anselm. If you do not believe me, search the barn. You will find there proof of what I say."

To Lily's immense chagrin, Titus intuited her betrayal. So deeply did he come to loathe her that when her father died a few weeks later, he did not come to offer his condolences. His resentment was not to be appeased. He had not so much as glanced at her for ten years.

"He has stayed on here as a living reproof, to rub salt in my wound. He is repaying me for the ill I have done him. His servility is terrifying, and it is directed against me. Do you know how many tears I have shed each time he obeys me? There they are, in the two salt cellars of this bust."

"Why then hold me responsible?"

"If Titus had not inherited your talent, if he had never seen your altarpiece and your salt cellars, none of this would have happened. This, Master Anselm, is why I hold such resentment against you. For ten years I have been cultivating it, though I must, by sniffing salt, remind myself why I hate you. Not only have I judged you, but sentenced you as well."

"What punishment do you intend to inflict on me?"

"You have already served your sentence. You thought you were turning your back on the past, but it has overtaken you. Did your offense not warrant ten years of forced labor in a salt mine?"

Master Anselm reflected at length before answering.

"Am I to understand that you do not intend to pay me for the work I have done?"

"Quite the contrary. This dinner, dear Master, was your salary."

The stone carver got up and bowed deferentially. Before leaving the table, he cast a final glance at Lily, as motionless in her chair as the bust upon the table.

"Resentment has not consumed you," he said. "Remorse has. By always looking behind you, like Lot's wife, you have transformed yourself into a pillar of salt."

Lily hung her head.

"I am the last of my lineage. I must look behind me, for there is nothing before me."

As he was about to leave the room, Master Anselm changed his mind and turned back.

"You have paid me in salt for ten years of toil, very well," he said through clenched teeth. "Be advised that I shall not be leaving empty handed. Titus has decided to leave Armagh. He is awaiting me on the Beaumont road."

Even once he had closed the door, Lily did not move.

Ursula and Perpetuity tiptoed into the dining room and bent over Lily's motionless body. They had waited until midnight for Her Excellency to ring for them to clear the table. Hearing nothing from the other side of the door, they finally became concerned and entered.

"Is she dead?" asked Perpetuity.

"No," answered Ursula. "She has only fainted."

"Thank God. I feared that she had succumbed to the same malady as the Rear-Admiral."

"Yes, praise be to God. Had that been the case, we would have had to salt her and bury her in the mine with the others."

"I'll get water to revive her."

"Why hurry?" whispered Ursula. "Let her marinate in her brine a while longer."

Perpetuity stared at her, perplexed.

"What are we to do while we wait for her to awaken?"

Ursula came over and took her by the arm.

"We shall use the opportunity to eat sugar!"

And the two of them hurried off to the kitchen with a hearty appetite.

THE END